The Lady in White

During the long tolls, they covered the east side of the graveyard. With the exception of the church bells, the place was quiet.

But when they turned the corner and headed down the west side, the dog suddenly sat down on his haunches and raised his muzzle to the sky.

An awful sound—part whine, part howl, part pulsating sob—suddenly filled the air and seemed to go on and on.

Only it wasn't the dog doing the crying. He was silent, his jaws closed.

"Look," Peter said, pointing. "She comes."

As Jennifer followed his pointing finger, she saw a white shimmering mist gathering above one of the horizontal gravestones, just at the stroke of twelve. Slowly it shaped itself into human form: a woman wearing a long, old-fashioned white dress, white gloves, white hat and veil. She had her black mouth open and she was sobbing loudly.

The ghost turned, pointed a long white finger at them, opened her shadow mouth again, and screamed. It was an awful sound, full of anger, fear, loathing, horror—and something else.

The
Bagpiper's
Ghost

TARTAN MAGIC

The Bagpiper's Ghost

Jane Yolen

MAGIC CARPET BOOKS
HARCOURT, INC.
Orlando   Austin   New York
San Diego   Toronto   London

Requests for permission to make copies of any part of the work should be mailed to the following address: Permissions Department, Harcourt, Inc., 6277 Sea Harbor Drive, Orlando, Florida 32887-6777.

www.HarcourtBooks.com

First Magic Carpet Books edition 2003

Magic Carpet Books is a trademark of Harcourt, Inc., registered in the United States of America and/or other jurisdictions.

The Library of Congress has cataloged the hardcover edition as follows.
Yolen, Jane.
The bagpiper's ghost/by Jane Yolen.
p.   cm.—(Tartan magic; bk. 3)
Summary: While in Scotland visiting relatives, thirteen-year-old twins hunting for ghosts in an old cemetery find big trouble when Peter is possessed by the spirit of a man who is determined to keep his twin sister from the man she loves.
[1. Ghosts—Fiction.   2. Magic—Fiction.   3. Twins—Fiction.
4. Scotland—Fiction.]   I. Title.
PZ7.Y78Bag   2002
[Fic]—dc21   2001006200
ISBN 0-15-202310-0
ISBN 0-15-204913-4 pb

Text set in Galliard Old Style
Display set in Goudy Medieval

H G F E D C B A

Printed in the United States of America

To Debby and Bob, Scottish hosts,
without whom, of course
and to Joanne Lee Stemple, who is a MacFadden

Contents

Tartan:
Plaid cloth.
In Scotland each clan
has its own distinctive pattern.

The
Bagpiper's
Ghost

One

Belief

I don't believe it!" Peter cried. His body showed his astonishment even more than his face, for his arms and hands were raised, and his feet did a noisy jig under the kitchen table. It was the most animated he'd been in days, even though he was clearly putting it on.

Spoon half lifted, Jennifer looked up from her porridge and stared at her twin. "You don't believe *what*?" Given that they had already had days of magic, it wasn't an idle question.

"Sun," Peter said, pointing out the window. "And no clouds, not even a hint. Must be my doing. I— Peter the Great." He waved his right hand as if he were royalty, something he'd just started that morning.

"I can believe sun," said little Molly, nodding so hard her little dark curls bobbed like Slinky toys.

"It's easy. Sun, sun, you've just begun. See?" Molly was in love with rhymes and repetition just now.

Peter turned on her. "Not in Scotland, it isn't easy," he told her. "Our sixth day on vacation here, and it's the first without a cloud in the sky. So I *don't* believe it. No—I take that back. It's *beyond* belief."

Jennifer shook her head. Sometimes Peter's sarcasm was over the top. Especially since they'd turned thirteen. It seemed impossible for one twin to hate the other, but lately Jennifer found Peter exasperating. Like the royal hand-wave thing. *Exasperating.* That was one of her mother's words, but useful.

"Nothing's beyond belief in Scotland," she reminded him, "now that we've found magic."

"We haven't *found* magic," Peter said. "There aren't bits of magic lying around that we just stumble over. No, wait a minute. I'm wrong. *You* just find magic, but it seems to avoid *me.* Maybe I have M.O." He glared at Jennifer, which made her feel uncomfortable.

"What's M.O., Peter?" asked Molly.

Jennifer was glad Molly had asked, because there was no way she herself was getting suckered into Peter's bad mood. Not with the sun shining and all.

He lifted his arm and shoved his pit toward his

little sister. "Magic odor. Like B.O., only worse. Smelly as well as repellent. Magic stays away from me."

Gran's white cat walked through the room and stopped to stare at Peter's uplifted arm.

Peter stared back and gave the cat the royal wave.

Jennifer sighed. "It's not like I'm *looking* for magic," she said. "Not like someone is leaving it on the ground . . ."

"My Pict stone was on the ground," said Molly, remembering their last adventure. She spoke with the flat-footed assurance of a four-year-old. "And *it* was magic."

"It *called* magic," Peter said, determined not to be outwitted by his baby sister. "It wasn't magic on its own. And Jennifer got to do all the cool stuff while we were out cold."

"Peter, why are you so determined to be a pain?" Jennifer asked.

"Pain in the rain. Pain in the rain," sang Molly.

She's exasperating, too, thought Jennifer. She watched as the cat gave them *all* a disgusted look and went through the cat door and out into the garden.

"But that's just what I was saying. It's *not* rain-ing!" Peter declared. "So you are all wrong, as usual, and I—Peter the Great—am not." This time he waved his arm grandly.

There was a roundness to his conversation. A great circle with no end. Jennifer recognized it just in time and bailed out.

"I'm going downtown," she said. "After breakfast. To Fairburn Castle."

"Me, too," Peter said.

"Me, three," added Molly.

"Mom!" Jennifer and Peter cried out together, their voices eerily similar. Mom, who had been reading a magazine in the other room, came in.

"We want to go for a walk," Jennifer said.

"Without the kid," Peter added.

"Jennifer and Peter want some twin time," Mom said to Molly. She opened her arms wide. "Besides, I need some Molly time, myself. After all, I scarcely saw you at all yesterday. And I missed you dreadfully."

"You mostly missed the excitement," said Molly. "And the magic. You went to Edinburgh. Without me. Me, me, me, and Mommy makes three."

"Two," Jennifer and Peter said together, but Molly ignored them, preferring her rhyme to reason. Or at least to math.

"That I did," said Mom. "Better tell me again."

"You missed the Pictish girl and the tallyman and the ..."

As Molly began the whole story, interspersing rhymed words in the telling, Jennifer and Peter slipped out of the kitchen.

■ ■ ■

In the living room, Jennifer turned on her brother. "I *don't* need twin time, and I *don't* want you with me," she said. "You're in a foul mood, and you're determined to ruin my day, too."

"But I'm in a good mood, Jen," Peter protested. "I am Goodness in person."

"No, you're not, Peter the *Great*." Jennifer put her hands on her hips. "You don't even sound like you anymore. So even if we go out the front door together, we are going to split up at the corner of Double Dykes Road." The tone of her voice gave him no room to argue.

She immediately felt bad about coming down so hard on him. After all, before they'd become teens, they'd done everything together. But now it was boy stuff and girl stuff, Peter stuff and Jennifer stuff. She wasn't entirely used to it and didn't entirely like it. The best thing about twins was being a single unit. Forever. But with Peter acting so awful . . .

"Nah—I'm sticking with you, kid," he said. "You seem to get in the thick of things here, and I wouldn't want to miss any of it. *This* time."

Jennifer wasn't sure he meant that admiringly. Lately it had been getting harder and harder to tell *what* Peter meant.

"Oh—all right," Jennifer said grudgingly. "But only if you lighten up."

"I will be lightness entire," Peter replied. "As light as—this sunny day!"

"There you go again," she told him.

He grinned at her, his old familiar grin, and suddenly all her anger disappeared.

Maybe, she thought, *I'm overreacting. Maybe Peter isn't moving away from me. Maybe I'm the one who is the problem.*

Just then a slim dog the color of ash pushed between them.

"Yer nae leavin' me behind. A day like this, the sun oot and all. That garden's nae big enough fer me. I want to spend the forenoon going my dinger."

Peter looked down at him. "Going your dinger? And what's that when it's in English?"

"I'll give thee *English*, laddie! Yer American language is nae English. And I am nae English, either. A Scot's a Scot fer a' that! 'Going yer dinger' simply means to go oot and aboot with vigor, ye young daftie."

Peter looked at Jennifer and shrugged. "Maybe we should all go our dinger!" He laughed. "And stumble over some magic while we're at it."

"Och, nae learned ought yet?" asked the dog, lying down and crossing his paws. "Dinna ye call for magic. It'll nae be pleased wi' the summons."

"Which," Jennifer pointed out, "is just what Gran would say if she were here." Gran wasn't Mom's real mother or grandmother. She and her husband were actually some older cousins who had helped raise Mom after her own parents had died in a car crash.

"And where *is* Gran?" Peter asked, attaching the dog's leash to the collar.

"The auld carlin is awa," said the dog. "Gone to Edinburgh, the auld gray toon. Something about a capped tooth."

"Or a gapped tooth," Peter said, winking at his sister. "Our gran being a witch, after all."

"*White* witch," Jennifer and the dog said together.

"Whatever." He shrugged, the smile gone from his face, and lifted the latch to the front door.

Jennifer's uneasiness returned, seeming to cloud what would otherwise have been a lovely day.

Two

Going Their Dinger

The door shut behind them with a satisfying *snick,* then Peter held out his hand as if expecting rain. He looked up, then grinned at Jennifer.

"Nae rain, nae haar," he said with an atrocious Scottish accent.

"Och, stick to the American," the dog said, disgusted. "No rain, no fog. Have a nice day." His broad American accent was just as bad as Peter's Scottish.

Jennifer ignored them both. If the two of them wanted to fight, she'd let them. She doubled the size of her steps and soon left boy and dog far behind.

Turning onto the cobbles of Double Dykes Road, she never looked back, though she could still hear them sniping away at each other. She liked going along on the uneven cobbles rather than the sidewalk. It suited how she felt.

Behind her came snippets of conversation.

"You wouldn't know a good day if it bit you," Peter was saying.

"Dinna talk to a dog aboot biting," came the response. "It might provoke mair than ye'd like, laddie."

"Try me, big nose."

"Two leg."

"One brain."

"Better than none, ye gormless American daftie..."

Just my luck, Jennifer thought. *Peter in an awful mood and a talking dog with an attitude!* She laughed out loud. "Now I'm rhyming like Molly." She began to walk faster.

The cobblestone path opened onto the road called Burial Brae and then onto the main street, and soon Jennifer was striding along. It almost seemed that by putting distance between herself and Peter and the dog, she could pretend she didn't know them. She even began to hum as she walked.

But at the first light, they caught up with her, still arguing.

Jennifer rounded on them both.

"Shut up or get away from me," she snarled. "Far

away." She was sure her face was as fiery red as her hair.

They fell quiet at once, almost as if silenced by a spell.

Of course, she knew no such silencing spells. As Gran would say, magic takes a lot longer to learn than six rainy vacation days in Scotland.

But, obviously, sometimes a snarl can serve just as well, she thought grimly.

The light changed, and Jennifer and Peter looked carefully both ways for oncoming cars. Magic gone awry was not the only danger here. Traffic in all of Great Britain drove on the left side of the street, not the right. Mom had drummed and drummed that into them. For their safety, they needed to check both lanes before crossing, even though they were teens and not Molly's age.

The road was clear in both directions. Jennifer bounded across, and Peter followed, yanking the dog along behind. No sooner were they all on the other side than boy and dog were at it again.

"Ye have a hard hand, laddie. Be careful I dinna bite it off."

"There's always muzzles, dog breath."

Jennifer turned and said very quietly to her

brother, "Peter, only someone who's got magic will even have a clue that the dog can talk. But everyone else will certainly wonder why you're holding such a one-sided conversation. So will you *kindly* please shut up." She glared at him. "You're embarrassing me."

Peter closed his mouth. His lips made a sharp, thin line, like a long dash in the middle of a sentence.

The dog, however, gnashed his teeth and growled, "Wee, timorous, sleekit, cowerin beastie," under his breath. He was caught up short when Peter gave his leash an awful yank.

"I'll *coward* you, you snot rag . . ."

After that, they were both silent.

And away from that trembling silence, Jennifer stalked stiff-legged, followed closely by her twin and the dog.

■ ■ ■

None of them said another word until ten minutes later, when they were in sight of Fairburn Castle, an impressive stone ruin with a couple of standing towers, and below ground, the remnants of a repulsive dungeon in the shape of an old bottle.

The dog spoke a careful, quiet sentence. "Do ye ken it's haunted?"

"What's haunted?" Jennifer asked.

Peter remained sullenly silent.

"The castle, ye doited lass," the dog began, before Peter yanked the leash again.

The dog growled, and a local woman and her two children stared at Peter.

He stared back.

Kneeling, Jennifer loosened the leash, and the dog grinned his toothy, slobbery grin at her.

"Aw, Jen . . ." Peter began.

"It obviously hurts him," Jennifer said. "And someone's likely to arrest you for animal abuse. They take that sort of thing very seriously here."

"Right on," the dog said in his bad imitation of an American accent. Then he gave Jennifer a long, slow, aggravating slosh across her lips with his tongue, laughing as she wiped the back of her hand across her mouth in disgust.

"Obviously it didn't hurt him enough," Peter grumbled.

Paying no attention to Peter's grumble or the dog's laugh, Jennifer stood and said, "You are *both* impossible."

"We only aim to please, Jen," Peter said, and winked at the dog, who—strangely enough—winked back.

"You . . . you . . ." Jennifer began.

"She likes us, dog," Peter said.

"She likes me better," the dog added.

"Does not."

Jennifer put her hands on her hips and leaned down till she was nose to nose with the dog. "You said a haunting. What . . . is . . . doing . . . the . . . haunting?" She separated each word in the careful way one talks to a child or a foreigner.

The dog turned his head and began scratching under his chin with a back leg. It was an insulting sort of scratch. He kept it up for a very long time.

"He doesn't know," Peter said. "He's made it up."

"He does know," said Jennifer.

"Doesn't."

"Does."

"Doesn't."

Another woman, with a redheaded child in tow, glared at them.

This time it was Jennifer who glared back.

"Before ye start up on World War Three," the dog

said, his scratching over, "I'll tell ye what haunts Fairburn Castle, if ye like."

"Yes," Jennifer said. "We like."

Peter nodded. "So speak, dog."

The dog's face got a sly look, and he shut his eyes.

Peter and Jennifer knelt, one on each side of him.

"Please," they said, one after another. "Please."

The dog's eyes snapped open. "Put that way, how can a bodie resist?" He grinned toothily. "The ghost's a lady in white. White dress, white hat with a veil, white gloves, and a white face, too. She bairges aboot the graveyard behind the ruins as if she's at some fancy-dress garden party, and not moldering in her grave."

They turned to him together.

"Have you—" Jennifer began.

"Seen her?" Peter finished.

Then they smiled at each other.

Still twins, then, Jennifer thought, enormously pleased.

Three
■ ■ ■ ■ ■ ■

Castle

Of course, I've seen her, that paidling maiden," said the dog. "Any *true* Scot can see her. And any other ghost. But if yer an Englishman or a villain—or a Campbell, of course—ye canna even get a glimpse." He shook his head, which made his ears flop.

Peter laughed. "Ah well, we're not English and we're not Campbells . . ."

"Or villains," Jennifer added.

Peter nodded.

"So . . ." Jennifer said carefully, "will *we* be able to see her?"

The dog shook his head from side to side again, ears flapping like wings.

"Pretty please?" Jennifer added.

The dog cocked his head to one side. "Not now, ye gormless lass."

The more the dog put her off, the more Jennifer suddenly wanted to see the Lady in White. "Why not now?"

Peter put out a cautionary hand. "Jen . . ."

But something—*Maybe something magic,* she thought—compelled her to ask again. "Well, why not?"

The dog grinned, as if in on some great joke. "Because it's daytime, ye coof."

"And ghosts don't come out in the sunlight," Peter added for good measure. "Only at night."

"Weel, of course at night. Dinna ye ken that she's a ghost, lassie?"

"We're not allowed to go out by ourselves at night," Jennifer said. "Not even at home."

"*Especially* not at home," Peter said.

The dog's toothy grin grew wide. His great pink tongue lolled out of his mouth like a dare.

"We could *sneak* out, I suppose," Peter said slowly.

"Peter!" Jennifer's voice registered shock. It was such an un-Peter thing to suggest. But she'd already thought the same thing.

Twins do.

"Tonight," they both breathed together.

"Good, then that's settled," the dog said, and began sniffing the curb, where other dogs clearly had been before him.

They let him do his business, then Peter pulled at the leash again, hauling the dog away from further investigations on the sidewalk or in the road.

"Come on," Peter said. "Let's check out the graveyard."

"For what?" the dog asked. "It's daylight, ye daftie."

Jennifer understood what Peter meant and—as usual—tried to explain it. "We need to see everything. Get the lay of the land. Figure out where all the stuff is." Her hands described large circles in the air. "For tonight."

The dog sat on his haunches, refusing to move. "Stuff?"

"Gravestones," Jennifer explained patiently.

"Pathways," Peter added.

"Bolt-holes, ye mean," the dog said. "Yer looking for escape routes. Hah!" He made a strange sound through his nose. "Ye scared wee bawties. Rabbits. Conies. That's what ye be. I had the right o' it before. Cowards, as the boy says."

Peter put his hands on his hips and leaned over,

speaking fiercely and directly into the dog's uplifted ear. "If we're going to come out here—sneak out here—in the middle of the night, dog, we're going to be prepared, understand? We're not entirely stupid, you know."

"Aye. Not *entirely*," the dog admitted.

"Or entirely powerless," Peter added.

"I'm counting on it," said the dog.

"What do you mean by that?" Jennifer demanded. "What do you know about this ghost that you're not telling?"

The dog snapped his jaws shut and shook his head, ears slapping madly at his nose. And though they begged and pleaded and finally threatened him, the dog stayed dumb.

■ ■ ■

So they made their way through the wrought-iron gates and into the castle graveyard without any help or advice or even any teasing from the dog, which—Jennifer thought—certainly made for a happy change.

The graveyard was very old, and scattered throughout with lichen-covered, rough gray stones from the sixteenth century on. Some of these stones stood upright, as if defying the weather; others tilted, as if they'd been defeated by the wind and by the years. And a few—thick and scarred—lay completely flat on the ground, as if they were the tops of casket lids.

In between the stones, what grass there was had been worn down by visitors until it was the same color as the soil.

A small church nestled amid the graves, its own stones a muted gray-and-yellow, the colors dulled even more by moss and lichen. Most of the stones in the church were deeply fissured by long weathering and the centuries, but a few of them seemed to have a different kind of covering, which stood in stark contrast to the rest.

When Jennifer remarked on this, the dog grunted, sounding remarkably like a pig.

"Harling," he said. "Harling protects the soft stane."

"How do you know that?" demanded Peter. "Mr. Know-It-All-Tell-It-Ever." It was one of his mother's favorite phrases.

"One of my masters was a stonemason," the dog answered carefully, then went dumb again.

"*One* of your masters? How many have you had?" Jennifer asked.

"Soldier, sailor, tinker, tailor," the dog offered, his tail beating in rhythm.

"And wizard," Peter reminded him. "Michael Scot was your master, too. Till Jennifer fixed that."

The dog's tail stopped wagging.

■ ■ ■

The most recent gravestone they found was dated 1927 and said simply LOST AT SEA.

"So no one is buried there," Jennifer said.

"Duh," Peter replied.

Jennifer felt her face go hot. Peter never teased like that. Even at home, surrounded by his friends, he always defended her. Once he had said that was what brothers were supposed to do.

Some brother you are now, she thought.

The dog smirked but refrained from comment.

Thankful for the dog's silence, Jennifer turned back to the gravestones. She found a name she recognized.

"Look, Peter—James Kirk, Captain, HMS *Bountiful.*"

"So the great man was a sea captain long before he led the *Enterprise*!" Peter commented. "Wonder if the *Star Trek* crew knew that he died in . . ."—he checked out the date, which had almost been erased by time—"1774."

Jennifer smiled a little at his joke, and peace was restored between them.

As if challenged by Jennifer's find, Peter began to scramble around the gravestones until he found some names they both thought downright silly: Zenobia McManners, Miracle Morrison, and Anache Dunrobin.

"Imagine going to school with them," Jennifer said. "They'd probably beg for nicknames."

"Zenny, Mirc, and Ana." Peter laughed.

"Anache is a boy's name," the dog put in dryly.

Right then the town-hall clock in the next street over rang out noon so loudly, Jennifer had to stick her fingers in her ears.

The dog suddenly jumped onto one of the horizontal tombstones, sat up on his haunches, and began to howl, a sound so full of pain it made Jennifer want to howl as well.

The dog's howling went on and on until the last bell died away. Then he jumped down and tugged at the leash, pulling Peter toward the east gate and home.

Peter tried to hold him back, but the dog—as if goaded by a hot iron poker—wouldn't stop. Peter had to either go with him or let him off the leash. "Jen—" Peter began to say, but she wasn't paying any attention. So, shrugging, Peter gave in and he raced away with the dog.

For a moment Jennifer wondered if the dog's sensitive ears had been hurt by the bells. But he had never complained before, and they had wandered through town when the clock had struck at other times. It was a puzzle.

Then, at the dying fall of the last bell, she thought she heard something else. Something very much like the long final note of a bagpipe, that low skirl of sound that comes as the pipes wheeze into silence.

She looked around but saw no one with pipes nearby, though, of course, she knew that bagpipes could be heard yards and yards—even acres and acres—away. *The Devil's horn,* Da called bagpipes. He didn't like them much.

Her eyes swept across the horizontal tombstone the dog had just vacated. Besides a name with the dates of birth and death, there was a poem inscribed on the gray stone. She read the inscription:

MARY MACFADDEN, GONE TO GOD,
MARRIED ONLY TO THE SOD.
IN THIS LIFE A MAIDEN BLEST,
NOW IN HEAVEN TAKES HER REST.
ERECTED BY HER LOVING BROTHER, ANDREW

"Well, Mary MacFadden," Jennifer whispered to the tombstone, "was it the bells that frightened the dog, the mysterious bagpipes—or was it you, you naughty dead lady?" She laughed out loud and then shivered, as if expecting an answer from beyond the grave.

But, of course, there wasn't any.

It was broad daylight, after all.

She hurried after Peter and the dog, finally catching up to them near Burial Brae.

Safely Home

They got home in record time. The dog kept the leash taut all the way and hadn't stopped to investigate any interesting smells even once.

When they turned into the lane at last and saw the cottage ahead of them, with its gray slate roof slumped like a farmer's hat, the dog began to babble aloud.

"By my fegs, I shouldna speak ill of the dead. I shouldna called her names in the boneyard. I shouldna—"

Jennifer interrupted. "I don't remember you calling anyone anything at all."

"Actually, he said the Lady in White was a 'paidling maiden,'" Peter reminded her as he undid the leash from the dog's collar. "Whatever that is. Sounds like a swimmer of some kind. Dog paddle, maybe." He smiled at his own joke.

It was so lame that Jennifer pretended not to notice and continued to stare at the dog.

"You didn't make much of a swear," she said softly. "At least it doesn't *sound* like much."

The dog had the grace to look down at the ground. "It means aimless and feckless," he explained. "But still I shouldna called her any such."

"Aimless," Jennifer repeated.

"Feckless," Peter said at the same time.

The dog nodded.

Kneeling, Jennifer took the dog's head in her hands. "Well, how is that so bad?"

"Och, child," the dog moaned, "a ghost is *never* aimless. It remains here on earth for a purpose. Even someone as gormless as an old dog should ken better than to say otherwise." He flopped down by the door and covered his head with his paws. "Oh my tail, oh my teeth."

"Then what *is* her purpose?" Jennifer asked, as much to herself as to the dog.

But the dog didn't answer, just continued to groan and moan.

It was many minutes before they could rouse him from his depression and get him to go into the house.

■ ■ ■

Everyone else was up and about by now, it being past noon. The house had taken on the atmosphere of a party, with music and games and food.

Gran and Molly were dancing on the thread-worn carpet in the Great Hall as Battlefield Band—a raucous Scottish rock-and-reel group—played on the radio. The sounds of bagpipe, electric piano, fiddle, and electric guitar filled the room as Molly twirled around and Gran clapped for her. The white cat lay on the sofa, its paws over its ears.

By the big window, where they could catch the light, Pop and Da were in the final stages of a chess game. By their elbows, cups of tea grew cold while they pondered their next moves. As far as Jennifer could tell, they were equally matched, down to a king, a queen, one rook, and one knight each. Pop was playing with the black chessmen, Da with the white. Neither one was laughing.

Through the window, Jennifer could see Mom in Gran's herbal garden, grooming the horse, Thunder, with a large brown curry comb. Thunder seemed to be enjoying himself. She couldn't say the same for her mother.

"*Hssst,*" Peter said to Jennifer, "let's get up to the attic while everyone is busy. We can make plans for sneaking out tonight without worrying about being overheard."

She nodded.

Peter turned and went up the stairs, taking the steps two at a time and quickly outdistancing Jennifer.

As Jennifer started up, the dog pushed in front of her. "Don't leave me behind," he howled as he scrabbled up the stairs after Peter.

"Damn dog," she whispered. Then she bit her lip. At home, swearing was a time-out punishment, but in Gran's house, you had to watch what you said even more. Here words had real power.

And power had a sneaky way of being tricky, as she had already found out in their first days in Fairburn.

■ ■ ■

The attic seemed drab and uninviting after the party downstairs. Shadows crisscrossed the floor-boards, and two flies buzzed at the windows. Old stuff was stored up here: worn-out clothes, antique books, broken golf clubs, parts of fishing rods, and lots of card games, none of which they'd ever heard of before arriving in Scotland—games like Patience and Happy Families and Bezique.

At home, they played Monopoly or Scrabble or Clue, or games on the computer, all familiar and comforting. The Scottish games were not only unfamiliar—some of them were positively dangerous, for they could call up strange and awful magic, and wizards, like the horrible Michael Scot.

Peter was already sitting on top of the old wooden trunk. Jennifer flung herself down on the tattered throw rug in front of him. The dog curled up by Peter's feet.

Suddenly the cat bounded up the stairs. It walked over to the dog and, as it passed by, lifted its tail.

"Och, ye deadly perfumer," the dog cried out. "Fowsome cat."

The cat smiled at him and walked over to Jennifer, then snuggled into her lap.

"What time do we go tonight?" Jennifer asked. The whole idea was beginning to make her faintly queasy, and her stomach had a hard knot in it, only she'd never tell Peter that. If she backed out now, Peter would accuse her of trying to hog all the magic again, and then was sure to go off alone. That, she felt certain, would lead to disaster.

"Everyone in the house should be asleep by ten," Peter said. "They're not much for late nights here."

The dog interrupted. "Never been out on a summer's nicht, I see."

"We told you we don't go out alone at night," Jennifer said.

"Och, weel, then yer not to ken aboot the licht," the dog said, then quickly added in explanation, "To know about the *light*," in an American accent that owed much to bad TV shows.

"The light?" Jennifer and Peter asked together.

The dog sniffed loudly and began cleaning between the toes on his right paw as if he'd said everything that needed saying. The air was thick with the twins' impatience.

The cat yowled, stretched, got off Jennifer's lap, and bounded back down the stairs as if it had heard enough.

Finally Peter couldn't stand the wait any longer.

"'*Ken aboot*' what light?" asked Peter.

The dog looked up. "Summer's licht," he said, then went to work on the left paw. "White nichts."

"Oh, that!" the twins said together.

"You mean how it's light well toward midnight," Jennifer said.

"White nights in summer," Peter added. "That's what happens in Moscow. We learned about it in school."

"If ye tak a gud look at a map, laddie, ye'll see where Fairburn is in relation to the Russias." The dog's face was incredibly self-satisfied.

"What do *you* know about maps?" Peter began, leaning slightly forward and staring down at the dog. "It's not as if you can read or anything."

"Er, Peter," Jennifer reminded him, "the dog lived a long time with the wizard Michael Scot. And the wizard had a map, remember?"

Peter seemed to blush slightly, though it was difficult to really be sure in the shadowy attic. "Sorry."

"No need, no need," the dog said, though his tail told a different story, thumping against the floor as if he was delighted to have forced the apology.

"So," Jennifer said quickly, "maybe we should wait till later, when it finally gets dark. Er... darker. Next month maybe?" By next month Peter might have forgotten the whole ghost thing. Or Jennifer might have learned some control of her American-style magic. Or...

"Weel after eleven," the dog said. "Coming towards twelve. It will be dark enough then."

"Midnight!" Peter breathed.

"How will we wake up?" asked Jennifer. "We don't dare let the alarm go off."

The dog grinned, showing all his teeth at once. "I'll wake ye both, my weans. Ye can be sure o' that!" Without another word, he stood and trotted down the stairs.

Jennifer looked at Peter. She knew what he was thinking, because she was thinking it herself: *How on earth would the dog know the right time?*

But Jennifer was thinking something else as well, something she knew Peter had no inkling of. She was thinking: *Why is the dog so eager for us to go find this Lady in White?*

FIVE
■ ■ ■ ■

Near Midnight

Jennifer lay in bed fully dressed except for her shoes, and tried to fall asleep.

The light kept peeping in from behind the gauzy curtains whenever they were stirred by the wind. Which was often. Gran believed in plenty of fresh air at night.

How can I go to sleep with so much light? Jennifer wondered, though, of course, she'd had no trouble any of the other nights they'd been in Scotland, falling asleep as soon as her head hit the pillow, exhausted from their adventures.

She worried about what lay ahead. What she had agreed to do. *It's stupid,* she thought. *And maybe even dangerous.* There was something the dog wasn't telling them. She promised herself she would not believe everything he said.

In the bed across the room, Molly started tossing

and turning. That was noisy enough. Then she started a series of sighs and snores. She sounded like the little engine that could, on steroids.

I'll never fall asleep! Jennifer thought.

Then she thought, *I'd better* not *fall asleep.*

And right after that, sleep grabbed her.

■ ■ ■

She was just dreaming of a particularly nasty fall into a filthy, smelly river that splashed cold water on her face, when she awoke with a shudder.

The dog was standing there, and right on time, sloshing a cold tongue across her face. The bedside clock said eleven-thirty.

She wondered how long he'd been drooling over her. Sitting up, she scrubbed at her face with the sheet.

"Is Peter awake yet?" she whispered.

"He's next," the dog replied in a low grumble.

"Maybe we shouldn't . . ." she began, but the dog was already out of the room.

As she grabbed up her shoes, she could hear the dog's nails clacketing on the wood floors. Next came a slurping sound, then Peter roundly cursing the dog.

Jennifer wondered briefly where he'd learned all those words, then worried about his swearing so much in Gran's house. She couldn't very well yell at Peter, though, not without waking up the entire house.

So, ignoring the two of them, she tiptoed down the stairs, being extra careful not to step on the third step down, which tended to creak.

A minute later, Peter and the dog followed.

They weren't so careful.

The sound of the protesting stair was loud enough to wake everyone in the cottage.

Or the dead, Jennifer thought, then shuddered, remembering where it was they were planning to go. She held her breath, listening hard.

Luckily, no one else seemed to have heard anything.

Down by the door, she put on her Nikes, kneeling to tie them quickly, as Peter and the dog came into the entryway.

Jennifer rose and put her finger to her lips, like Mrs. Flight, their homeroom teacher, did at the beginning of each school day. *"Shhh."*

Peter stopped in his tracks and looked guiltily over his shoulder, but the dog growled a low rumble.

"Dinna caution me, lass. Teaching yer granny to suck eggs."

"What do you mean by that?" Peter said.

"I mean, ye toom-headit colonial, that I already know how to be quiet and need nae teaching. Any more than ye need to teach the auld besom of the house how to fix breakfast." The dog's indignant voice rose to a growl.

"*Shhh*," Jennifer said again, louder, and beckoned them to the door.

They stood still for a moment and listened to make sure no one was coming to check up on all the noise, but the only sound they heard was the ticking of the grandfather clock in the hall.

And—Jennifer thought—*the beating of my heart*.

Then Peter grabbed the leash from the umbrella stand and snapped it onto the dog's collar. At the same time Jennifer pulled the great oak door open—another awful sound—and closed it quickly after them. The catch falling into place sounded as loud and as final as a bomb blast.

■ ■ ■

They tiptoed across the cobblestone road. Or, at least, Jennifer and Peter did. The dog walked normally, his toenails clacking at each step.

When at last they got to the main road, Jennifer sighed. "You two are the *noisiest*—"

"Not me—he's the one," Peter said, gesturing to the dog.

"*He* is," the dog replied.

"You're worse," Peter said, "clicking away on those stones."

"And what about that groaning stair in the house?" the dog snapped.

"That was you, not me," Peter said.

"Was not," the dog answered.

"Was, too!"

"Will the two of you shut up!" Jennifer said in a loud, exasperated voice, no longer caring who heard.

"*Shhh!*" Peter and the dog said together, and the dog grinned.

It was not a good start.

■ ■ ■

At eleven-fifty, the roads in and out of the town were very quiet. Hardly a car went by. The sky glowed with a strange yellow-gray light, and there were long shadows everywhere. It was an eerie in-between time; not day, of course, but somehow not really night, either.

If there's magic about, Jennifer thought, *this would be the moment for it to appear.* Her stomach ached as if she'd eaten something that didn't agree with her.

"It's near midnight," the dog said. "We'd best hurry."

Jennifer suddenly wondered what was so darned important about midnight, why the dog was chivying them through the empty streets.

As if—she thought suddenly—*we are sheep and he the sheepdog heading us toward the fold.* It was an uncomfortable thought.

"How do you know it's near midnight?" asked Peter. "You don't wear a watch."

"Got ears, haven't I?" the dog said. "Got eyes."

"Got tongue, will travel," Peter added under his breath.

"I heard that, ye coof!" said the dog.

"Oh, for Pete's sake!" Jennifer said.

Nevertheless, they hurried.

■ ■ ■

By the time they were at the castle, the church bell was striking midnight.

This time, the dog seemed almost unworried about the sound of the bells. And yet he had been so worried about them at noon. *Or,* Jennifer thought, *worried about something else.*

She was just about ready to say something, when Peter, who had been fiddling with the latch on the wrought-iron gate, finally got it open on the third stroke of the hour.

"Come on in, you guys," he said.

The three of them went inside, the dog careful not to touch the gate because cold iron is harmful to magical creatures. Peter closed the gate after them, checking the latch twice to be sure.

"So no one going by will wonder why it's wide-open," he told them.

Jennifer nodded. "Good idea." *Though,* she thought, *we didn't pass a soul coming here. So why should we worry about anyone coming along now?*

She started toward the gravestones, Peter by her side.

The fifth stroke had just rung, a long, low, mournful sound.

When Jennifer looked back, the dog was standing by the gate, only a few steps in.

"Come on," said Jennifer. "We need you with us."

"Someone has to guard the way for ye," the dog said. But there were tremors running up and down his back, like little worms beneath the skin.

"Who's the bawtie now?" Peter crowed.

"No one calls me a bawtie!" the dog answered. He marched over to them, rather stiffly, in time to the sixth and seventh tollings of the bell. The whites of his eyes were showing, and the ruff of his back was way up. "But dinna put the blame on me if somebody's needed at that gate later on."

"No one's blaming you for anything," Peter said.

But Jennifer was not letting the dog off that easily. "Except for tricking us into coming out here."

"No tricks. No tricks," the dog cried. He stood suddenly on his hind legs and turned around three times. Then he dropped down again on all fours and repeated, "No tricks from me!"

■ ■ ■

During the long tolls, they covered the east side of the graveyard. With the exception of the church bells, the place was quiet.

"Silent as a tomb," said Jennifer, then bit her lip at the unfortunate phrase.

But when they turned the corner and headed

down the west side, the dog suddenly sat down on his haunches and raised his muzzle to the sky.

"Don't you dare—" Jennifer warned him.

But her warning came too late. An awful sound—part whine, part howl, part pulsating sob—suddenly filled the air and seemed to go on and on.

Only it wasn't the dog doing the crying. He was silent, his jaws closed.

"Look," Peter said, pointing. "She comes." There was a strange triumph in his voice.

As Jennifer followed his pointing finger, she saw a white shimmering mist gathering above one of the horizontal gravestones, just at the stroke of twelve. Slowly it shaped itself into human form: a woman wearing a long, old-fashioned white dress, white gloves, white hat and veil. She had her black mouth open and she was sobbing loudly.

"The Lady in White," Peter whispered. Even in the half-light, Jennifer could see he was flushed, and his face, for a moment, was almost unrecognizable with his excitement.

"Mary MacFadden," Jennifer whispered back. She'd recognized the stone above which the ghost hovered.

The weeping ghost and the bell stopped at the

same time, so the sound of Mary MacFadden's name seemed magnified in the sudden stillness. In fact, her name seemed to crystallize as it left Jennifer's mouth, hanging in the air before Jennifer like an icicle off the lip of a statue.

The ghost turned, pointed a long white finger at them, opened her shadow mouth again, and screamed. It was an awful sound, full of anger, fear, loathing, horror—and something else.

Longing? Jennifer thought, shivering, and not—she guessed—from the cold.

The dog, though, evidently had no such thoughts. He flung himself away from Peter with such strength, the leash left a rope burn on Peter's palm.

"Ow," Peter cried, bending over to catch hold of the end of the leash. "Come back, ye daftie."

But the dog was too quick. In twenty steps he bounded to the closed gate and frantically wriggled underneath its lowest bar, yelping as the cold iron burned a thin stripe down his back. Then he galloped down the road toward the cottage, leaving the children alone in Fairburn Castle cemetery with the angry, ghostly Lady in White.

SIX
■ ■ ■

Bagpiper's Ghost

What do we do now?" Jennifer asked, trying to get her hands to stop shaking. Her stomach seemed to have made its way to her throat. Yet, somehow, her voice was remarkably calm.

Finding a ghost had sounded like an exciting idea when they'd first talked about it, a way of letting Peter share some of the magic that seemed to infest this part of Scotland. Then when she had had second thoughts, the excitement of the idea had given way to fear.

Now it was just plain scary.

"Follow the dog's lead?" Jennifer answered her own question. "Let's get out of here. The dog seems to know something about her that we don't."

She pointed at the ghost, who was drifting closer and closer to them, the tatters of her long white dress looking more and more like a shroud the nearer she came. Her face was dead white, and her features were made of shadows. Yet as awful as she was, she was beautiful. Jennifer felt sorry for her.

"Shouldn't we find out what she wants first?" asked Peter in a calm, sensible voice.

"What she *wants*?" Jennifer's hands trembled like an old woman with a palsy. Since she couldn't stop her hands from shaking, she put them palms down on Peter's shoulders, to steady herself. When she felt how rigid his shoulders were, as if he was working hard at holding himself together, in a funny way that made her feel better. He was as scared as she was.

"What her *purpose* is," Peter said slowly, pushing each word out carefully. "Like the dog said. Remember? A ghost remains here on earth for a purpose."

Jennifer remembered. And she tried to be brave. Really she did. But with the ghost only five gravestones away, she no longer cared about any purpose—other than to get out of there and head for the ironwork gate.

She turned and ran.

Peter passed her in six steps and was at the gate

before she was. He was about to fling it open, when he stopped short and Jennifer crashed into his back.

"What do you think you're—" Jennifer began.

He pointed.

On the street right outside the gate stood a very tall, and very dirty, bearded man carrying a large set of bagpipes. He wore a kilt of no discernible color, a soiled shirt, and a piece of tartan slung over one shoulder. His long socks were pulled all the way up his shins. The handle of a dagger stuck out of the top of his right sock. There was a sword in a sheath hanging from his belt.

"Who is he?" whispered Jennifer into her brother's ear.

But before Peter could answer her, the piper set the tip of the chanter to his mouth and began to blow.

After the first awful groanings, the bagpipes wheezed into life, and the piper began a tune they both recognized—from one of their mother's recordings. It went on and on.

"It's 'Ye'll Tak the High Road.'" Jennifer whispered the words of the song as their mother had taught them. "'Ye'll tak the High Road and I'll tak the Low Road? Peter—can we stop him? He'll wake the entire town."

"Wake the toon?" Peter whispered back. Then he cleared his throat several times as if something were caught there. "Good. We need all the help we can get with that thing back there." He glanced for a moment behind Jennifer at the ghost, who was slowly drifting toward them, then turned his attention back to the piper.

The powerful piping continued, and yet not one single light had come on in the nearby houses.

Just then Jennifer felt something deadly cold pass by her shoulder. *Winter in summer,* she thought. When she turned her head to see what it was, she found the Lady in White standing right beside her. The cold was pouring off her like an air-conditioning unit. Jennifer was too frightened to make a sound, not even to warn Peter, who still stared, as if entranced, at the piper.

"What do you want?" Jennifer said slowly, quietly, almost mouthing the words.

But the Lady in White didn't seem to notice her. Like Peter, she had eyes only for the piper.

"Iain . . ." the Lady in White cried in a voice thin

as air. She held out a trembling, translucent hand. "Iain, luv, ye've come hame to me."

The piper's fingers stopped moving, though the pipes still groaned out a few notes by themselves. He lifted his mouth away from the chanter, smiled sadly, then reached a hand toward her. "Mary Mac-Fadden, I've come hame. But too late, too late, dear heart," he cried.

"Never too late," returned her answer, as soft as the air between them.

Their hands quivered on either side of the fence, but it was clear that neither of them dared pass the barrier of the ironwork gate.

"Peter," Jennifer cried, "*he's* a ghost, too."

Peter didn't move.

Jennifer added, "The dog was right. That's their *purpose*. To be together. But they can't cross cold iron. It will burn them. Open the gate for them, Peter. Open the gate."

As if only now realizing his sister was behind him, Peter turned around and glared at her, his eyes wide and shining in the half-light of the Scottish midnight.

Jennifer had never seen him look like this, not

even the time she'd accidentally broken his precious CD player.

He's mad, she thought.

Not furious mad.

Crazy mad.

"Awa!" he shouted at her, his voice deep as a man's. "Awa, sister. There's nae a thing here fer ye noo."

"Peter?" Jennifer cried. *"Peter?"*

Peter stared at her, uncomprehending, eyes wild. His mouth had twisted into an unfamiliar grimace. Deep lines suddenly appeared on either side of his nose, sloping downward, as if he were more accustomed to frowning than smiling, as if he'd suddenly put on twenty heavy years.

Jennifer knew with sudden, awful certainty that what was standing in front of her was no longer entirely her brother. *But who is he?* she wondered.

"And who are ye, lass, standing betwixt me and my ain?" not-Peter asked. He pushed her aside, saying, "Oot, oot the way." Then he addressed the ghost beside her. "Act the lady ye are, Mary MacFadden."

"No lady, brother, but a woman in luv."

"Luv? Hah!" Peter laughed, but not in his usual light way. This was a hard, stony laugh, as if the one doing it was unused to humor. "How oft hae I told ye, a common soldier like Iain McGregor is nae fer ye. He's but a mere impoverished Catholic mischant."

The Lady in White knelt before him. "The heart has nae religion, brother."

"Then train the heart, woman," Peter said, folding his arms over his chest. "Yer a MacFadden. And the MacFaddens dinna marry McGregors."

"Why not?" Jennifer asked, but no one seemed to know she was there.

"He is a man wi'oot honor," Peter continued. "McGregor may have wooed ye, but he never luved ye. If he had, he wouldna gone off to pipe a tune for that Italian upstart wi'oot writing ye a word o' farewell."

It was Peter speaking but they were not Peter's words. Not with that accent. Not with that information. Jennifer knew this, but she didn't know what to do about it, so she turned and went up to the ghost of Mary MacFadden, who had thrown her white hands over her white face and was weeping as if her heart was breaking.

"Don't let him talk to you that way," Jennifer whispered. "You don't have to stand for it."

As if Jennifer's permission was all she'd been needing, Mary MacFadden took her hands away from her face. "Bonnie Prince Charlie is nae Italian upstart, brother, but the son o' our king from across the sea. And Iain was a patriot to go to his aid, though it cost him his life at Culloden."

From beyond the gate, the piper's mouth gaped open. He made a sound like a man hit in the stomach. "Cost me my life?"

Mary MacFadden glanced over at him.

The piper put his hand out and cried, "Nae dead at Culloden, sweetheart. Nae dead."

When she didn't answer, he cried out again, "And did ye nae get the message I left ye by yer brother himself?" He looked at her with eyes full of love. "Ye ken I canna write."

Mary MacFadden turned to Peter. "Did ye lie to me, then, Andrew? Did ye tell me an untruth? That's a sin, Andrew MacFadden. The Lord doesna luv a sinner. And ye the kirk's ain minister."

Peter's face got dark, heavy. His mouth twisted as if the words he said were pushing out through a screw hole. He raised his hand as if to strike her. "Nae sin, sister. Merely an omission. It was fer yer ain sake."

Jennifer could scarcely believe her brother would say any such thing. She had to remind herself that he was this Andrew MacFadden now, not Peter. He was speaking like an eighteenth-century man, not a boy in the twenty-first.

The Lady in White winced and shrank away from the raised hand. But it did not stop her response. "If ye were truly thinking o' my sake, Andrew, ye'd hae thought o' my heart, too. Which belongs to Iain." She wrung her hands again. "But always, Andrew, it's been yer ain comfort ye hae been worrying aboot. Ye wanted me to yersel, to mak yer tea and keep the hoose and all fer free till the end o' yer days."

"Ye'll nae be speaking to yer older brother like that, Mary MacFadden," Peter said, his mouth still in that peculiar twist.

"Peter!" Jennifer cried. "You're *my* brother, not hers." But it was as if he did not hear her.

The Lady in White stared at him, shadow tears running down her face. "Older by but a minute, Andrew, and me fast on yer heels oot o' the womb."

Jennifer gasped. "You're *twins*? Maybe that's why the dog brought us here. Twins to twins at midnight, some sort of strange, dark magic. Don't you see?"

They both turned to stare at her then, and at that same moment a ribbon of sun touched the horizon.

Mary and Iain disappeared at once.

And Peter, like a puppet with its strings suddenly cut, collapsed at Jennifer's feet, face down, and didn't move.

SEVEN

To the Rescue

Peter!" Jennifer knelt down and started shaking him. But though his eyes were open, the pupils had rolled up, and it was as if he stared at her with all-white eyes.

Jennifer glanced around the graveyard, then across the road, hoping to see someone who might help. There was an arrow of light along the horizon, though she knew it couldn't be more than one in the morning. But just then the church bell rang four times.

"Four?" she whispered. "Four already?" She hadn't thought the argument between the MacFaddens had taken that long. Then she realized that within a bubble of magic, time had no meaning. She looked back down at her brother and shook him, but still he didn't wake.

Putting her head to his chest, she heard a steady *thump-thump-thump* and was comforted by it. He didn't need CPR or anything like that, which she could do if she had to, having learned it in health class. But he was in some sort of a coma or shock. She put her arms around his shoulders and held him as if he were a baby, rocking him back and forth.

It's my fault, she thought, *all my fault.* And then, as an afterthought, she added, *And that stupid dog's!*

For a long moment she wallowed in her misery. Then she realized that whining about whose fault it was did not help the situation.

"Do something," she told herself, and then she began to scream.

"Help!" she cried. Even to her own ears, her voice sounded thin and weak. "Help!" This time she was louder. But the nearest houses were blocks away, and anyone asleep or with the windows shut wouldn't hear her, anyway.

I'll carry him to one of the houses, she thought.

She tried lifting him up in her arms, but even though they were twins, he was a lot heavier than she was.

"I can drag you," she told his unconscious body.

But then she remembered the videos they had watched in school about what to do in case of an accident. *Never move someone. Wait for the ambulance.* That had been drilled into them, because moving someone might only make things worse.

But was this an accident? Or was it something else?

"Where is the magic now that I really need it?" she whimpered, miserable and guilt-ridden, even though she knew that what feeble magic she had was untrained and untested and probably unmanageable. It was American magic, after all, and they were in Scotland.

"I'm sorry, Peter," she whispered, gently laying him back on the cold ground. She meant she was sorry to have gotten him into this in the first place, sorry to have been a bad sister, and sorry to leave him, even for a moment. "I have to go get help." Then she stood and looked around.

Across the street and one block down was a row of darkened houses. She could run there and knock on the door until someone woke up, and then ask to use the phone. Mom had taught them that the emergency code here wasn't 911 but rather 999. Someone in one of those houses might even lend her blankets to cover Peter until other help could get there.

Or she could run back to Gran and Da's cottage, about a ten-minute trot, less if she ran flat out. Maybe that would be better. After all, this was a matter of ghosts, of magic, not an accident. So who would know better about what to do than Gran?

Just as she was trying to decide which way to go, she heard a strange, light clopping sound racing down the street. Turning, she saw an odd, wonderful sight.

Nightgown flapping about her bare legs, a plaid shawl around her shoulders, white hair streaming behind, Gran was galloping toward the graveyard on Thunder's back.

Being a magic animal, Thunder couldn't wear iron shoes, of course, which was why his hooves made such a peculiar, light sound on the paved road.

Behind them, as gray as a ghost, tail firmly between his legs, came the dog.

"Gran!" Jennifer called, waving an arm. "Over here!"

Gran gave the horse a quick, sharp touch with

her bare heels and leaned over his neck. Gracefully he leaped over the gate with about a foot to spare.

Jennifer's mouth dropped open. "Gran!" she said in an awed voice. "I didn't know you were a rider."

Sliding off the horse, Gran landed with a grunt in a squatting position. Putting her hand to her back, she straightened up slowly, as if counting each vertebra.

"My blue ribbons have all been put awa," she said. "I've nae been riding fer years." She grimaced. "My knees are too auld fer this," she added. "And the rest o' me as well."

"Oh, Gran," Jennifer cried, giving her a big hug. "Thank goodness you're here."

"Och, lassie, what have the pair o' ye been up to noo?"

Jennifer burst into tears. "It was all my fault. All of it."

Gran's face grew serious as she looked down at Peter, still stretched out on the ground. "I'm sorry to be so slow getting here. The cat warned me something was afoot, but didna know what. Then the dog came hame and hid himself fer a while, greetin and carrying on. It was a while before he came creeping into my room to whine aboot his ain guilt. Seems there's plenty o' that gaeing around."

Jennifer wiped a hand under her drizzling nose and nodded.

Gran continued. "When I could finally make sense oot o' what that greetin teenie was blethering on aboot, he told me he had introduced ye to the Lady in White. And somebody else beside. 'An auld friend,' he said. 'Nae gud,' I told him, 'messing aboot wi' the spirit world. Dangerous,' I said. 'There's nary an auld friend when yer speaking aboot ghosts.'"

"*Two* somebody elses, Gran," Jennifer said. "If you count Peter."

"Count Peter? Why should I count Peter?"

They knelt down beside Peter, and Jennifer tried to explain to Gran exactly what had happened, in as few words as possible.

Gran put a hand on Peter's shoulder to wake him, but to no avail. Even a shake didn't work. A hard shake. So she gave a nod to the dog, who crawled over on his belly and lay down by Peter's side, snuggling up close. Then Gran took the shawl from her shoulders and put it over them both.

"The lad's breathing well at least," Gran said in a sensible voice. "So it's nae immediately threatening to his life, whatever it is. And the dog will keep him safe." She raised a hand, forestalling any questions from Jennifer. "Nae magic, my dear—but body warmth till we can sort this. Quick, though, tell me everything noo. *Everything*. Dinna leave a bit of it oot. Wi' magic o' this sort, one never kens what is important at the first."

So Jennifer explained about the Lady in White whose name was Mary MacFadden, and about Iain McGregor the piper, and how her brother had not passed on some sort of message. When she got to the part about Peter speaking in Andrew Mac-Fadden's voice, Gran interrupted.

"Possession, of course." Her face looked angry, and her lips were set so tightly against each other, they might as well have been sewn together.

"Well, *I* knew that," Jennifer said, disappointed. "It's like in the movie *The Exorcist*. Peter spoke in this funny voice and didn't seem to really know me. Only he didn't throw up on me or turn his head around or anything gross like that."

"Never believe what ye see in the cinema," Gran

said. "And only half o' what ye read in the books." She knelt again and felt Peter's forehead. "No fever. That's good." Then she looked up. "Anything else?"

Jennifer shook her head. "No, Gran, I've told you everything."

"Everything?" Gran stared into Jennifer's eyes as if seeing right inside her.

Then suddenly Jennifer remembered. "They were twins, Gran. Mary and Andrew. Twins, like Peter and me."

"Ah." The old woman breathed the word. "Doubles the trouble, that does. No wonder he could slip into Peter's flesh wi' such ease. That and the fact that Peter has been a vessel before."

"A vessel?" For a moment Jennifer was confused. Her mouth gaped open.

"When that wizard Michael Scot used him so sorely." She reached into her sweater pocket and drew out a handkerchief. In it were the ashes of the wizard, which Gran carried with her day and night.

"Oh, that," Jennifer said.

"Being possessed is like having a bairn, a baby," Gran said. "Stretches the body in ways ye'd never believe."

"Oh, Gran," Jennifer said, horribly embarrassed but fascinated at the same time.

Gran smiled at her, but grimly. "It'll be harder getting him oot noo. Because of the time before, when he hosted the spirit o' Michael Scot."

" 'Him'?"

"That other twin." Gran got up slowly. It was clear that kneeling was not something she did with any ease.

"Should we call for help?" Jennifer asked. "Nine-nine-nine?"

"The Fife ambulance wouldna ken what to do wi' him," said Gran, her hand on her back. "Nor the constabulary. This needs magic, not medicine."

"What kind of magic?"

The horse, Thunder, shook his head, and for the first time that evening spoke in his plummy voice. "To find that out will take a bit of research, child."

As usual, he was right.

EIGHT

A Long Sleep

They brought Peter home, slung over the horse's back like an old sack. As they walked along, the horse and its burden seemed to glow. Jennifer put her hand up to the glow, but it had no warmth. And no cold, either. It was simply there.

She wondered about that glow for a minute, especially when policemen in a police car waved at them but didn't stop to offer any help.

"Does that glow make Peter and the horse invisible?" she asked as the horse turned onto the cobbled street leading to their house.

"Invisible to everyone except those who have magic in the blood," Gran said. "Good for ye, lass, for noticing at last."

"I *noticed* immediately, Gran. It just took me till here to figure out *what* it was. But you and me and the dog—why aren't we invisible, too?"

Gran sighed and held up the forefinger on her right hand. "Working an invisibility spell is tiring enough over two. Nae need to extend it where it's not wanted. Why waste magic, lass? We must conserve what power we have to rescue yer brother. So, as far as the rest of the world sees, we're but a wee lass and her gran oot walking the dog."

Tiring, indeed, Jennifer thought. *Gran looks exhausted.* There were deep circles under the old woman's eyes and a sharp crease across her forehead, like a knife's slash. Or like the shadow of a knife's slash.

Still she asked, "At *four* in the morning, Gran?"

"And herself in her nightie," the dog put in, but at a look from Gran, he shut up.

"It's *five* o'clock noo," Gran said.

At that very moment, the nearby church bell began to toll five long, slow notes.

■ ■ ■

They dragged Peter upstairs between them, which wasn't easy. He hung like a deadweight. The dog made the going even harder because he kept tangling in their feet.

Jennifer was so disgusted with the dog, she aimed a kick at his side, but he dodged it easily.

"Didna I fetch the auld carlin fer ye?" he said, a whine in his voice.

She ignored him after that, concentrating instead on getting Peter to his room and into bed.

While Jennifer took off Peter's shoes, Gran got a "clout"—as she called the washcloth—and a large bowl of warm water. Then she began washing Peter's face.

"Will that dispossess him?" Jennifer asked.

"Nae, lass, it's just to clean him up. I dinna want yer mother seeing him this way. Too many questions mak fer too many answers, as my ain mother used to say."

"Then what's to be done? About the possession, I mean," Jennifer asked.

"Likely he'll wake up himsel again," Gran said. Her voice sounded positive, but there was a strange darkness in her eyes. "Often these things are but a moment lang. Fer example, if a ghost in possession o' a human body has nae mair to say, it'll go back to its burial wi'oot needing a helpful push." She wrung out the cloth and stood up. "Here, lass—

dump this water into the sink and set the clout on the basin. I'm fer bed."

Jennifer did as Gran asked, then went back to Peter's room. Lying still on the bed, he suddenly looked younger than she did. And unprotected.

I will protect him, she thought fiercely, lying down at the foot of the bed.

She meant to stay awake, like a medieval knight at a vigil, or a cop on a stakeout, but the long night had exhausted her, and she fell fast asleep, lying as if dead for seven hours.

■ ■ ■

Waking at noon, Jennifer was surprised to find herself in her own bed. The clock seemed to shake its fingers at her, turning over one minute, then the next. She stretched lazily and tried to remember why she was so tired.

All she could think of was the strange dream she'd had. About a Lady in White and Gran jumping a fence on horseback.

"Oh no!" She sat bolt upright in bed. It *hadn't* been a dream.

Leaping up, she ran into Peter's room, and there

was her mother sitting and reading a paperback novel by Peter's bedside. The white cat was snugged on the pillow by his head.

Mom looked up gravely when Jennifer came in. "Hi, sleepyhead. Feeling all right?"

"Me?" Jennifer shrugged. "Sure."

Mom shook her head. "This whole family seems to have a sleeping sickness today."

"Is Peter . . . ?" Guilt stopped the rest of what Jennifer was going to say, like a cork in a bottle.

"I think he caught something yesterday. We haven't been able to wake him, though he's been tossing and turning and calling out in his sleep. I've sent for the doctor. Do you know they still do house calls here? Thank the Lord for that." She brushed a hand softly through Peter's hair.

"A doctor?" Jennifer knew a doctor wouldn't help at all. Gran had said Peter needed magic, not medicine. She sat down heavily by his feet.

Her mother continued. "I was worried about you, too. Found you right here, lying at the bottom of the bed. Your father had to carry you into your own room, and you're no lightweight anymore." She smiled and set the book down on her lap carefully, but her voice was tight with worry. "What's this all about, Jen?"

Jennifer suddenly realized that parents sometimes had to be protected from the world. What they *didn't* know couldn't hurt them, she reasoned.

So she said, just as carefully, "I heard Peter crying out in the middle of the night, and I was afraid he'd wake Molly." That wasn't exactly a lie, just not the whole truth. "So I came in to see what was wrong. He was having a bad dream or something. I settled him down, then curled up here, waiting to see if he was going to be all right. I guess . . . I guess I fell asleep."

Her mother gave a tight little laugh. "Twins!" She touched Peter again as if to assure herself he was still there. "And you weren't just asleep, Jen. It was as if you were dead."

Jennifer gave a tight little smile. "Well, I'm not dead. See." She opened her arms.

Her mother sighed, an uncharacteristic sound. "Gran sat with you until about an hour ago. For an old woman, she's got an inexhaustible supply of energy."

Remembering Gran on the horse, Jennifer said, "She sure does."

"I'm going downstairs to phone and see if the doctor's on his way. Will you stay with Peter a little while? I don't want him to wake up alone. Then I'll make you something to eat."

"Not hungry, Mom."

"Nonsense. You *will* have something to eat. Porridge. That's just the thing. And it'll take only a few minutes to make." She put the book and her glasses on the bedside table, reached over and picked up the cat, then straightened slowly, suddenly looking like an old woman herself.

■ ■ ■

It was another fifteen minutes before the white-haired doctor got there, examined the still-sleeping Peter, and left a bottle of pills by the bedside.

"One when he wakes, and one every six hours after." His voice was pleasantly English.

Mom nodded and sat down again by Peter's side. Pop sat at the foot of the bed. Exchanging dark looks, Gran and Da stood in the doorway. In the hall, Jennifer shifted from one foot to the other. Only Molly wasn't with them. She'd been sent off to a neighbor's to play with their children for the day.

"Best to get her out of the way," Pop had explained.

Jennifer thought they should have sent the dog with her, for he lay whimpering by the bedside, as if by remaining close to Peter he might undo all the damage he'd done taking them to the cemetery.

She felt like doing the same.

Gran and Da accompanied the doctor downstairs, their voices floating back up to Peter's room.

"They *will* overdo when they come on vacation," the doctor said to Gran and Da. "Youngsters always think they're indefatigable. Especially American youngsters."

"Nonsense," Gran said as Da closed the front door behind the doctor. Jennifer could hear the latch click into place. "Pills and all. It's nonsense."

"Is it magic then, Gwen?" Da's voice asked.

"Aye, 'tis."

"There's been an awful lot of that aboot since the bairns arrived," he added. "First Michael Scot, then that lassie from the past, and noo this."

Gran answered, "The twins seem to call magic to them. They dinna mean to, but it's in the blood."

Hearing that, Jennifer shivered.

"It's too much fer them," Da said sternly. "They being Americans with no sense aboot it, no control."

"I'll see it's stopped," Gran said. "Or finished."

Jennifer started down the stairs just as Da went out the door after the doctor. Gran looked up at her and nodded, as if giving permission for her to leave Peter for a little while.

"What's *indefatigable*?" asked Jennifer when she got to the bottom step. "Undefeated?"

Gran grinned. "Something like that, lass."

Then they went in to eat their porridge, which—as Pop liked to say—was the real magic that stuck Scotland together.

NINE

Studying

The porridge was nicely warm and just a bit chewy. Jennifer tackled it as if she were starving.

"Losh me!" Gran said. "Yer hoovering that up instead o' eating it. Slow down, lass, slow down. Let's think aloud aboot first steps while we're breakfasting. Though…" She shook her head. "Breakfast at one fair beggars the imagination."

Jennifer stopped shoveling the porridge into her mouth for a moment. "Well, if Peter is possessed, Gran, shouldn't unpossessing him be our first step?" She whispered and looked hastily around in case her mother or father might overhear them.

"Powers, nae!" Gran said. Carefully she set her spoon down in the bowl and whispered back. "First we must make sure he's still possessed and not just sleeping off his exhaustion. Being possessed takes a lot of energy."

"And if he's still . . ." Jennifer took a deep breath. "If he's still Andrew MacFadden?"

"Och—I've never liked the MacFaddens," Gran said. "Uppity folk, indeed. Always looking down their lang noses at the rest of us. There's plenty in this toon still. I made some calls while ye slept on, to find oot what I could about Andrew and Mary. The MacFaddens dinna like to give oot gossip, but I phoned a friend at the Hall of Records. Seems she died young."

"We already knew that," Jennifer said.

Gran nodded. "Aye, we did. But what we didna know is that Andrew MacFadden lived to a ripe old age, married late, and had children and grand-children, though he never got over mourning his twin. Put up a memorial to her inside the little church. Made oot a charity in her name. Och, *he* was the one possessed, that Andrew MacFadden. Probably had bad dreams all his life."

"Well, what if he's still inside Peter?" Jennifer asked. "And using Peter to bring back the sister he mourned forever?"

"Then we have a *big* problem," Gran told her. She stood. "However, first things first, lass, and this we canna rush. If MacFadden is still here and using puir Peter, we must ken what kind o' ghosts we're dealing with." She raised one finger and shook it at Jennifer. "In matters o' magic, knowledge is the most important beginning step, as surely ye have discovered by noo."

"But, Gran," Jennifer whined, "we have to do something *now!*"

Gran shook her head. "Rushing aboot is an American disease. We Scots ken that slow and steady in the ways o' magic is best." She turned toward the door and then said over her shoulder, "I'll get my book."

Jennifer pushed the porridge bowl away. *How can I even think about eating with Peter lying upstairs possessed? What kind of a sister am I?* And then she had another thought: *What kind of brother was Andrew MacFadden, treating Mary that way?* It made Jennifer hate him. She ground her teeth together and stood, planning to go up to check on Peter once more.

Just then Gran came back. "This is the volume on ghosts," she was saying, holding out a large tome bound in dark red leather. "Sit doon, Jennie. Study comes from quiet contemplation." Sitting back down at the table, she patted the chair next to her. "Ye'll tak the notes." She handed Jennifer a pen and a piece of notebook paper that was longer and narrower than the kind Jennifer was used to at home. "Come, lass, sit."

Jennifer sat.

Opening the book, Gran ran her finger quickly down the table of contents. "Glaistigs—nae, they're female and shape-changers. And our bonnie lad is neither a dog nor a lass."

Jennifer put a hand over her mouth to keep from giggling. *Peter as a girl? Or a dog?* The idea would have been sidesplitting—if the situation weren't so serious.

"And . . ." Gran continued, "they're mischief makers besides. This is nae such a one. Nor is it green ladies, either."

"Well, what about ladies in white . . . ?" Jennifer asked.

"Notes, my little lass," Gran said. "Unless ye've a better memory than mine."

Jennifer dutifully wrote down NOT and under it put *glaistigs* and *green ladies,* though her spelling was atrocious.

Keeping a finger carefully on her place in the book, Gran looked at Jennifer. "Noo aboot that white lady—colors are important in magic, child.

White is nae green, nae matter how hard ye squint." She turned back to the book. "And we're nae dealing with the banshee or the caoineag. All they do is moan a bit and flap aboot, warning o' a death to come." She shivered. "Horrid folk."

Jennifer shivered, too, but dutifully wrote down the names under the NOT list, spelling them as best she could. "Are there lots of different ghosts in Scotland, Gran?"

"Hundreds," Gran said with grim satisfaction. "Nae—thousands. Sometimes the unshriven dead all march together in a great lang parade, one after another, their winding clouts flapping in the wind. Then it's called the Sluagh."

"Sloo-ack? Should I write it down?"

Gran nodded. "Sluagh."

Jennifer scribbled the name.

"The death march o' ghosts," Gran continued. "And those o' a superstitious nature never leave a window open on the west side at night because o' it."

"Is Peter's room on the west side?" Jennifer asked in a horrified whisper. "He always sleeps with his window open."

Gran threw her head back and laughed. "That's

nonsense aboot the west window. Mere superstition." She laughed again. "Dinna ye be believing it. Superstition is fer folk who dinna ken much aboot real magic."

Jennifer gaped.

"Ye must ken what's true and what's only toom-headit," Gran cautioned.

"Toom-headit?"

"Empty-headed nonsense," Gran said. "So we crack the books, as ye say in America. Though a crack in a magic book is nae a good thing."

Sighing, Jennifer said, "Green ladies and white ladies and the Sluagh and superstitions. I don't know *what* to believe anymore, Gran." She was horrified to find she was crying.

Gran placed a hand on Jennifer's. "That's why study is important if ye have magic in ye, Jennifer. And right noo, we must study as hard and as fast as we can. Fer young Peter's sake. And fer our own."

Jennifer smiled through her tears. "Don't you know—I'm on vacation, Gran. School's out. I'm done with studying for the summer."

"A bodie's ne'er done wi' studying," Gran said. But she smiled back at Jennifer to show she got the joke.

Ten

The Low Road

The kitchen's gotten a wee bit close," Gran said suddenly. "A body can scarce breathe in here."

That was exactly how Jennifer had been feeling, too: choked up, as if lying under a heavy blanket on a hot day.

"Let's tak the book into the garden," Gran said, getting up from the table. "There's naught like the smell o' summer herbs to clear a bodie's head."

Jennifer got up eagerly and followed her out.

"The wee beasties can help, too," Gran said, nodding at the horse and the white cat. The dog, who'd been kicked out of Peter's room, was there as well.

"Not so wee," Jennifer told her, and they both giggled.

Dog and horse raised their heads at the laughter, but the cat paid no attention to them and headed across the rolled lawn to the summerhouse.

"Beasties often sense ghosts where we humans dinna feel a thing," Gran said.

That made the dog grin, his tongue flopping out like a piece of used bubblegum. "See—sometimes I can be o' help."

"And *sometimes*," Jennifer hissed at him, "you make a mess of things and then run away at the first sign of trouble."

The tongue disappeared. As did the grin.

"No apologies?" Jennifer asked the dog.

He was silent.

"And no explanations, either?"

"Dinna ye forget how he came to get me," Gran told her, her forefinger raised.

"And took his own good time about it," Jennifer reminded her.

"Och, we'll get to apologies and such once we have young Peter back," Gran said, looking down at the dog. "Meanwhile, Thunder here, having spent a lot o' centuries with that great and wicked sinner Michael Scot," she added, nodding at the horse, "may have some insights fer us."

At that, the horse started to paw at the ground, as if embarrassed by the praise, but Gran made a *tsk* sound with her tongue, reminding him that he was too close to her herb garden. So he stood still, a small tremor like a waterfall running across his flanks.

Jennifer and Gran sat down at the garden table. Gran got a strange look in her eyes, as if she had suddenly gone blind, her eyes opaque as marbles.

"Gran!" Jennifer cried, and put her hand on Gran's, which was cold, and marblelike as well. It was terrifying.

Slowly Gran's eyes seemed to change back, the hand under Jennifer's getting warm again.

"What just happened to you?" Jennifer whispered hoarsely.

"Thinking," Gran said, but the way she said it indicated that it was no ordinary kind of thinking; it was something deeper, harder, dangerous.

"Thinking about what, Gran?"

"About the dead." Gran's voice was dull.

"For a minute..." Jennifer said quietly, "for a minute I thought you *were* dead."

Gran smiled at her and opened the book. "Sometimes to truly ken a bodie, one must *be* that bodie."

"I don't understand," Jennifer said, shivering. But she did.

It was the dog that put it into words. "The auld

carlin means that to ken the dead, ye must become dead yersel."

Gran saw the stricken look on Jennifer's face. "Nae *really* dead, my dearie. Just magically so."

"Is that why the cat has run off to the summer-house?" Jennifer asked.

Gran nodded.

"You...you don't expect me to try that dead thing, too?" Jennifer said in a small voice.

"You are not ready for any such," Thunder told her, but gently. He shook his great head, and a waft of horse smell, warm and musky, enveloped them.

"The dead," Gran said, ignoring the horse, "dinna always ken themselves passed over. And so they canna pass on. They're tied to the place o' their greatest grief. Mary MacFadden to the grave where she wept herself to death. Iain McGregor to the home where he left the young woman he luved. And Andrew MacFadden..."

"But why isn't Andrew a ghost, too, Gran? Why did he have to possess Peter in order to be seen and heard?" In her eagerness, Jennifer leaned forward, her hand on the red leather book. "And will he leave Peter's body quietly?"

"If your gran knew the answers to all that," Thunder said, once again shaking his massive head so that his mane looked like dark waves, "she'd be up there in Peter's room right now."

Gran slid the book away from Jennifer. "The horse is right. I dinna have all the answers. But this I ken—if Andrew MacFadden doesna gae quietly noo that yer brother has had a long sleep, we have real trouble."

"Realer than this?" Jennifer asked.

Gran nodded. "I suspect that Andrew MacFadden is too angry fer peace, too guilty fer a quiet haunting, and that his heart is the size o' a wee hard stone. But all my blather is nae more than wind in the heather, lass. We must follow the book to ken what we must do next." She patted the cover of the red book and then opened it.

"But, Gran—" Jennifer started, thinking that the one thing no one had mentioned yet was the dog's role in the whole disaster. "What about the—"

Anticipating her question, the dog ran off into the far end of the garden, his tail between his legs. However, Gran was so deep in study, she didn't seem to notice, and so Jennifer reluctantly let the question go.

■ ■ ■

They kept on with the red leather volume on ghosts well through the afternoon, Jennifer taking notes as they went along.

Twice Da stuck his head out to check up on them. The last time, he said he was going out for a walk and would pick up Molly on the way back.

Gran nodded and waved him on, but never lost her place in the book.

After that, they worked their way through the customs of sitting up with or "waking" a corpse before a funeral, death lights, and phantom funerals. They read about deaths—by hanging, by drowning, and in battle.

"There seem to have been an awful lot of battles in Scotland," Jennifer said, scribbling furiously, the pen making blots on the page. "And an awful lot of ghosts."

"Ghosts on the High Road and Low," Thunder put in.

The dog, who had been slowly inching back toward the table, suddenly sat up and began singing in a high nasal voice, "Ye'll tak the High Road and

I'll tak the Low Road, and I'll be in Scotland afore ye..."

Putting her finger in her ears to block the awful howling, Jennifer turned to Gran. "Can't you stop him?"

Gran lifted the point finger on her right hand and the dog was silenced. "That's a wee bit interesting, Jennie. Let's think more upon it. It's a bit o' ghost lore we've not come upon in our book yet. The Low Road—that's the spiritual path along which a ghost might return to the place of his birth."

Thunder whickered softly. "The song comes from two friends, supporters of the King Over the Water, who were captured by the English. Only one of them ever escaped. The other was hanged."

"Good," Gran said, nodding at him. "Good."

"Hanged." Jennifer shuddered. And then she gave a start. "That's it!"

They all stared at her.

"There's nae a bit o' hanging in our nicht adventure," Gran said.

"No, no," Jennifer said. Her hands were making circles in the air and her voice rose excitedly. "Not

the hanging part. The song. That's what Iain Mc-
Gregor was playing on his pipes."

"Was he noo?" Gran leaned forward. "Are ye certain, lass?"

"I'm *positive*, Gran. I sang along with him."

"And ye've only just remembered?"

Jennifer hung her head.

"Never mind, lass, never mind. This is why we
gae aboot this magic stuff slow and steady." Gran
smiled at her. "How much did ye sing?"

Jennifer shrugged. "Not much. I only remembered the first few lines." Then an idea came to her.
"You know, I bet Iain McGregor *did* die at that
battle after all."

Gran leaned forward. "Go on."

Jennifer didn't need much encouragement. Somehow everything suddenly seemed to fit. "Well, what
if he died, and then he took the Low Road home,
but he just didn't *know* he'd died. You said, Gran,
that sometimes dead folk don't realize they've passed
over. Suppose Iain McGregor didn't know—but
somehow his pipes did. Could that be right?"

Smiling slowly, Thunder showed a remarkable set
of large yellow teeth. He whinnied with pleasure.
"She's a smart girl and may be on to something."

Gran smiled, too. "So noo ye ken that slow study does reveal all."

"Well, it wasn't something we actually found in the book, Gran," Jennifer said.

"One thing leads to another. All is connected," the old woman told her, emphasizing what she was saying with her finger upraised.

Bounding the last few feet toward them, the dog cried, "But I was the one! *I! I!* Had I nae sung the song..." He suddenly sounded a great deal like Molly, who was only four years old and therefore had an excuse for such behavior.

"Sung it? More like you *howled* it." Jennifer had to shout to be heard over the dog's commotion. She was disgusted with him—furious actually—because *he* was the real cause of Peter's possession. If the dog had never mentioned the stupid ghost in the first place, hadn't insisted on their going to the graveyard at midnight, hadn't left them when the ghosts appeared, they wouldn't have gotten into such trouble. Then she remembered her own role in the disaster and realized that the dog was not alone in creating it.

"I'm sorry," she whispered. "Of course, it was you who thought of the song."

Suddenly her mother burst out into the garden. "He's awake," she cried, looking both happy and frightened. Her hair was standing out around her head, a dark halo of curls, and there were unshed tears pearling in her eyes. "Peter's awake. But we can't make out a single word he's saying."

ELEVEN

Madhouse

They went into the house—all but the horse, of course—and Jennifer galloped up the stairs two at a time.

"Peter!" she cried. "Peter!"

Bursting through the bedroom door, she stopped short. Pop was sitting on the bed, holding on to Peter's shoulders as if trying to calm him.

Clearly Peter was not being calmed. His face was drawn up in a strange grimace, and he was cursing steadily, but in a broad Scots accent.

"Ye blind doited bodie, ye dorty man, are ye fou or fowsome?" Peter cried, his arms flailing.

Pop held on to Peter, but he looked up at Jennifer with such agony on his face, she wanted to cry.

"What's he saying?" Pop asked. "I can't understand a word of it."

Gran bit her lip, then took a deep breath. "He

said that yer a blind, foolish, stubborn man. He asked if ye were just drunk or an obscenity."

Peter smiled. Or rather the man in Peter's body smiled. It did not improve his looks. "I never told her. She never asked. And what was I to tell her, anyway? Truth is nae absolute. Nae if it's meant to hurt a bodie. 'In the stane a token of luv,' he said. The fool. The doited fool. Luvstruck and gawping. *Who's to ken it?* I thought. 'Three from the bottom and four above.'" Peter began to laugh with the other man's voice. "Three from the bottom o' hell, I tell ye. Four above."

"*Who* is he?" wailed Mom.

"*What* is he?" Pop's voice echoed her.

"Confused," Jennifer said.

"Mad," the dog muttered, though Mom and Pop didn't understand him.

"He's a *teenager*," Gran said with finality. "That's the very definition of madness." She raised her right finger and pointed it at Peter, who went dead quiet. Then she turned to Mom and Pop. "Gae downstairs, both o' ye, and leave Peter to me. I've handled worse."

Mom hesitated.

"Gae!" Gran said. "Noo."

"Okay," Mom answered, her voice as unsteady as her legs, "but I'm calling the doctor."

"Tell him to come wi' a lang needle," Gran said.

As Mom, supported by Pop, went out the door and down the stairs, the dog added, "And a lang spoon."

"*A lang spoon?*" Jennifer asked.

Gran looked at her. "He means a *long* spoon." She pronounced it carefully. "When supping wi' a Fifer, 'tis said, one should bring a lang spoon."

Jennifer raised both her hands as if admitting defeat. "I don't get it."

"The dog's guessing Brother Andrew was born and bred here in the Kingdom o' Fife. And when dealing with a Fifer—so they say—one has to be a wee bit extra careful, because a Fifer is that canny, that smart."

"But aren't *you* a Fifer, Gran?" Jennifer asked.

Gran laid a finger beside her nose. "Who better to deal with one?" She turned back to Peter, who still sat, unmoving, on the bed. "That small hold spell will do fer noo. But we haven't much time, lass. Andrew MacFadden has nae gone quietly awa back to his ain grave after the boy's lang sleep, as I'd hoped. If we canna get Peter back in his ain body by tomorrow, Andrew will stay in control o' it forever."

"Forever?"

"Aye. The longer a ghost is in a body, the less it wants to leave. We have another twenty-four hours at best."

Jennifer took a deep breath of air. "And at worst?"

"In Bedlam—the madhouse," the dog added morosely. "Who's to walk me then, I ask ye?"

Gran rounded on him, glaring. There were little spots of color on her cheeks. "I'll put *ye* in the madhouse if ye dinna shut yer cake hole."

Jennifer had never heard Gran so angry.

The dog shut up, closing his mouth so quickly his teeth made a loud snapping sound.

"Now what?" Jennifer asked.

"Noo we wait till evening," Gran said.

"More waiting? But Gran, if time is important, why don't we *do* something? Now?" Jennifer was appalled at how whiny she sounded, but she couldn't stop herself.

Gran put her arms around Jennifer and said quietly, "Because we need the dark, lass. Andrew Mac-Fadden came in the dark, and he'll gae oot the same way. It's the summer solstice this eve, and ye two are twins, as the MacFaddens were. Twins hold great power every day, but more so on the solstice. Something has begun that's stronger than my magic, I fear. So we wait, lass. We wait. But only till the dark."

"Ye doited carlin," the dog dared in a gravelly voice, "it hardly gets dark at all this time o' the year." Then he stood trembling, clearly expecting some awful fate to fall upon him because he had spoken out again.

This time Gran ignored him. After all, he *was* right.

* * *

The same white-haired doctor arrived within fifteen minutes, carrying his little black bag. He gave Peter a shot that put him out cold immediately. One sigh and he was gone. Then the doctor gathered the rest of the family downstairs.

The dog came, too.

"It's probably just a hormonal change," the doctor said, nodding at Pop. "Peter's going from a boy to a man. Sometimes it happens this way. The body is set for a gradual change, not for things to happen all at once. And poof!" The doctor's hands described an explosion.

The dog put his paws up over his ears, mumbling, "*Poof* is nae a medical term."

Silently, Jennifer agreed. She wondered about the doctor's competence. Besides, Gran had said this wasn't a problem that a doctor could solve.

The doctor continued, leaning toward Mom as he spoke. "I'll come by and check up on young Peter tomorrow. But if he's still much the same, I'm afraid I'll have to recommend hospitalization. I don't like to do that with tourists. I'd rather send you all home, where your family doctor can see to him. But if he's incapable of traveling..."

Mom and Pop nodded, their heads going up and down as if on strings.

Jennifer felt cold inside, then hot. The cold was her guilt, sitting like an iceberg in her stomach. Like the iceberg that sank the *Titanic*. The hot was her temper. It was a volcano. She was furious with the doctor's smug account. Hot and cold. The room suddenly seemed to be spinning.

Maybe I'm going crazy, too, she thought. But she knew she was as sane as could be. It was the rest of the world that had suddenly become the madhouse.

She thought carefully: *We have to get Peter back tonight.*

Tonight.

Because if the doctor takes Peter away from here—from Fairburn and Fife—he'll never get better. He really will *be Andrew MacFadden, that awful, lying man.*

Forever.

Twelve

Runaway

Dinner was a sad affair. The roast was burnt, the potatoes undercooked, the green beans over-cooked into a gray mash, and there was no pudding.

It didn't matter, of course.

Jennifer pushed the potatoes around her plate with her fork and couldn't eat a thing.

Mom and Pop sat with glazed looks on their faces, and Da's normally sunny smile was turned down into one of the dourest frowns imaginable. Gran was clearly thinking about something other than the meal in front of her.

Only Molly had any appetite.

And the dog.

The dog waited patiently under the table for scraps. Jennifer knew he'd have a lot to eat soon.

Afterwards dragged by as well. Jennifer tried a couple of games with Molly, because none of the grown-ups wanted to talk at all. They played Stone, Scissors, Paper, with the cat sticking her paw out as if playing with them every third round. They attempted several verses of the hand-clapping "Miss Mary Mack." They even tried some card games. But Jennifer couldn't get up much enthusiasm for any of it, and Molly, sensing something wrong, asked if she could just watch TV, instead. Jennifer was grateful to stop playing.

In fact, they were all in a state of tremulous listening, as if expecting any minute to hear Peter start ranting and raving and speaking in a foreign tongue again.

Only Molly—happily watching a game show she didn't really understand—seemed blissfully unaware of the danger.

■ ■ ■

Those hours between dinner and bedtime seemed endless.

Endless and full of endless light.

At last Molly, who had fallen asleep on the sofa, was carried up to her room by Pop around nine o'clock. There Mom undressed her and tucked her into bed.

Jennifer followed, took off her own shoes, and lay down fully dressed on top of the covers. She got out the piece of paper from her pocket and attempted to make sense of her notes, in case there was something important there: *glaistig, green ladies, banshee, sluagh*. None of them seemed to be part of the spell. Besides, she doubted she'd got any of the spellings right and wondered if spelling mattered.

"Of course, *spelling* counts," she told herself in a loud whisper, "in *magic*!" She smiled a little and thought how Peter would have loved the joke. "Spelling counts," she said again. Somehow it no longer seemed so funny.

"Mmmmmm," Molly called out, mostly asleep. "Jennnnnn?"

Jennifer looked over at her little sister. The last thing she needed was to wake Molly and have to explain a lame joke. "Everything's fine, Molls," she whispered. "Just fine."

Though, of course, *nothing* was fine.

Peter was possessed by some eighteenth-century liar and twin abuser, and it was all her fault.

Her fault.

And the dog's.

Molly turned over and went right back to sleep, making her little *pop-pop-pop* snore.

Shoving the paper back in her pocket, Jennifer tried to fall asleep herself. Really she did.

But no such luck.

She tossed and turned and ended up with the sheets wrapped around her neck in a stranglehold. Having to untangle herself woke her up completely. She knew she would never fall asleep now.

So she got off the bed and tiptoed into Peter's room.

Still knocked out by whatever the doctor had injected into him, Peter was snoring lightly. He looked no different from her old familiar brother. No sign of the awful Andrew MacFadden anywhere. But Andrew MacFadden was still there. Jennifer knew that for certain.

Dead certain.

Or certainly dead, she thought.

Peter turned over heavily but did not waken.

"Oh, Peter," Jennifer whispered, "don't leave me. Don't leave me and become some dried-up old Fifer who lies to his sister and keeps her from her own true love."

Peter opened his mouth, then closed it again without a sound.

"You're my best friend, Peter," Jennifer said. "You're my twin. We were together before we were with anyone else. We belong together now. Come back. Come back."

She tried not to sound sappy. Peter hated sappy. But there were tears in her eyes.

Something like a shadow of an answer passed across Peter's face. But still he slept.

Kisses always work in fairy tales, Jennifer thought. She bent over and kissed him on the forehead.

He didn't stir.

"Oh, Peter," Jennifer cried again. She couldn't stand feeling so helpless, so she went back to her own room. This time when she lay down on top of the covers, she fell instantly to sleep and slept without dreams.

■ ■ ■

At eleven-thirty something woke her. Some strange sound. A scraping, a grunting, a cascade of foreign language.

She got up slowly, still half asleep, and walked

out into the hallway. Looking out over the half bal-
cony that Gran called a minstrel's gallery, she saw
that the front door of the house stood wide-open.

"Peter?" she whispered.

No one answered, so she went to check up on
him. In the half-light, she saw the bed was empty.

Quickly she checked in the bathroom down the
hall.

He wasn't there, either.

She ran down the stairs. A washcloth lay by the
open front door.

"Peter . . ." she called, loud enough to be heard
outside, but not so loud as to wake the house.

Still no answer.

She ran outside, paying little attention to the way
the pebbles hurt her bare feet.

The road was empty.

Why didn't the dog bark? She thought. *Where's
Gran? Why didn't she wake me? What should I do now?*

She took a few tentative steps on the road and realized that going barefoot would slow her down.
So she went back into the house and found her
shoes. Then, just to be sure, she checked Peter's
room again.

A strange, muffled sound came from the closet.

Opening the door, she found the dog tied up, a gag made out of a sock tight around his jaws.

Quickly she untied him.

"Oh my ears and tail, he swicked me," the dog moaned. "Swicked me and tricked me. Aye, he's a canny one."

"Peter?" Jennifer asked.

"Nae—that spoacher, that minister, Andrew Mac-Fadden," the dog said, shaking himself all over. "The one who stole Peter's body fer his ain."

The noise brought Gran into the room.

"Hsst," she said, "is Peter gone?"

Jennifer nodded.

"And got oot the door how?" Gran looked puzzled. "I thought the cold iron latches would stop him."

"So that's why the washcloth was by the front door," Jennifer mused. "He must have used it to shield his hand."

"I said he was canny," the dog put in.

"Then we must follow," Gran said. "Nae one minute must be lost."

"Now you're rushing?" Jennifer asked.

"Noo it's dark," Gran said solemnly. "And dark is

the time to deal wi' ghosts. I was just aboot to wake ye, lass." She was already dressed, her pocketbook clutched in her right hand. When she saw Jennifer staring at it, she smiled dourly. "Fer my magicks, Jen. My unguents fer emergencies. And my hankie."

"Fer nose drips," the dog commented.

"Are you *kidding?*" Jennifer began, then shut up at the look Gran gave her. She remembered what was in that hankie now—the ashes of the wizard Michael Scot. "Well, what about Mom and Pop and Da?"

"Asleep," Gran said, her right finger making a circle in the air.

"And Molly?"

Gran made a grimace. "Likewise."

"And if they wake?"

"They willna," the dog answered for her. "The auld carlin's bespelled them."

Gran looked grimly satisfied. "We need nae screamin' and carryin' on when there's real magic work to be done. And there's nae an ounce of magic in any o' them. Except perhaps the wee lass. But she'll be nae gud wi'oot her sleep. Come." She cocked her head, listening for a minute, then put her fingers to her mouth and let out a shrill whistle.

Thunder met them at the open front door

Gran hoisted Jennifer onto the horse's back, then, with a strange little leap, mounted behind her.

"Oof," Gran said. "Getting too auld fer sech."

"Could have fooled me," Jennifer whispered.

The horse turned and set off down the cobbles, the dog trotting by his side. Even without metal shoes, Thunder seemed to make an awful racket clattering along, but Jennifer knew that since no one in the house would wake, it didn't matter.

At the corner, the white cat waved them off with its long tail.

They were in a full gallop on Double Dykes Road before Jennifer realized they were riding with neither saddle nor reins. Trembling, she leaned over Thunder's neck and grabbed hold of his mane.

"Not so tight, girl. I will not let you fall," the horse called to her.

But still she held on.

As they turned onto the main road, they were suddenly passed by a single car.

"Ride 'em, Granny!" someone shouted out the car window, then the car careered out of sight.

After that, the street was empty.

Thirteen

Stones

The horse's feet cloppetting on the pavement and the steady rocking movement of the gallop had a lulling effect, and Jennifer almost fell asleep again.

But suddenly the dog bayed. "See him, see . . . see!"

Jennifer startled and at that moment felt more awake than she'd ever been in the past two days. Leaning forward, she sighted down the road over the horse's head in the gloaming, the semidark, and saw Peter just turning onto the path that led to the graveyard gate.

"Gran!" she cried, turning her head to tell the old woman behind her.

But Gran had already seen.

"Gae to it, horse," Gran urged.

As if he had wings on his feet, Thunder flew

down the street with a gait as soft and as fast as a Thoroughbred's.

Peter would have gotten into the graveyard before them, but he was stopped at the iron gate by the great ghostly figure of Iain McGregor. The piper had pulled out a wicked-looking sword and wouldn't let Peter past.

"Oot o' my way, McGregor," Andrew shouted, waving his hand dismissively at the big man.

"Ye'll gae no further in, Andrew MacFadden," the piper boomed. "Nae on this nicht or any other, till ye mak amends for the wrong ye did to me and my Mary." The sword inched toward Andrew's chest.

"Can a ghost sword harm a real person?" Jennifer asked, looking over her shoulder at Gran.

Gran's voice whispered in her ear, and it seemed laced with fear. "I dinna ken fer certain, Jennie lass. A sword meant to harm a ghost *might* harm a mortal boy if he houses that spirit." She shook her head. "I canna say."

If Gran doesn't know, Jennifer thought, *then no one knows.* In a panic, she tried to shout Peter's name, to call him back to himself, but the sound that came out was thin and without power.

The horse came to an abrupt stop right by the

wall, and Jennifer tumbled forward onto his neck. She clutched him tight, her hands still twisted in his mane.

Gran slid off Thunder's back with an ease born of old habit. "Come, lass, we've work to do."

Sliding off after her, Jennifer cried out to the piper, "Don't hurt him. Don't hurt the boy. He's not who you think he is. He's not really Andrew MacFadden." She felt the familiar comfort of Gran's hand on her shoulder and continued. "He's my brother. My *twin* brother."

The piper's sword stopped just short of Peter's throat, holding there. His grip was firm.

Just then, gasping for breath, the dog limped the final block toward them. Somehow he'd gotten a pebble lodged in one paw as he was running, which had slowed him down. Moaning and gabbling to himself, he managed to reach the gate, where he sat down on his haunches and worried the pebble with his teeth.

"Stanes," he mumbled. "I hate them. A stane in the paw is the worst."

The word pierced Jennifer like an arrow.

"'Stane,'" she whispered. "It means something. Gran?"

Gran looked at her and saw that Jennifer was wrestling with some memory. She reached into her pocketbook and hauled out the hankie in which the wizard's ashes were tied. She held it to Jennifer's ear as if it were a seashell that could sing a song of the sea.

"Remember," Gran said.

"Stane," Jennifer repeated. Then her eyes got bright. "That's it, Gran. Something Peter said about a stane. Before the doctor got to the house. When Peter was gabbing and babbling. Only I can't quite get it . . ."

It was Gran who remembered. "'In the stane a token of luv. Three from the bottom and four above.'"

"What's a stane?" Jennifer asked.

"A stone," the dog said, looking up at them.

"Then maybe," Jennifer said thoughtfully, "maybe Iain's message was about something left for Mary in a stone somewhere." She took the hankie from Gran and turned to the piper. "What token did you leave, Iain McGregor? What stane did you leave it in?" She held the hankie toward him.

The big man shook his head, as if clearing it. "There's so much time twixt me and my hame." His face twisted in agony. "I...I canna recall." He pushed the sword closer to Peter's throat, and the tip drew a red line down the skin. "Can ye tell us, ye auld liar?"

Trembling, Peter shook his head. "Never!"

The piper's face got grim, but Jennifer cried, "Don't kill him. He's the only one who knows which stane the token is in." She shook the hankie at them.

"I'll die first," Peter said in Andrew MacFadden's voice.

"Ye coof, yer already dead," the dog said.

"I'll find the stane," Jennifer promised. "Let me try." She handed the hankie back to Gran and, without another word, squeezed past the piper with his sword, past her possessed brother and her grandmother and the dog. "Stay here and make sure he doesn't hurt Peter. I'll find that token. I promise." She pushed open the ironwork gate just a sliver and slipped through.

"I ken ye will, lass," Gran cried. "This feels richt in my bones."

"Ye have till midnight," warned the piper. "That's all I'll offer ye."

"But that's only minutes away," Jennifer said.

"Midnight," Gran repeated. "On solstice eve. O' course. O' course. A time o' power and the exact time ye first encountered these fey folk."

"Don't worry, Gran. I know I can find it." Jennifer turned to look at the graveyard behind her, and her heart sank.

There were stones everywhere. Gravestones and headstones, a stone wall, and stones in the church ruins as well. How would she ever find the one stone that was three from the bottom and four above?

"From the bottom of *what*?" she whispered. "And above what?" She shook her head miserably. "Mary MacFadden, your brother's a pig!"

As she spoke the name, a white mist rose from one particular gravestone. Slowly it formed into a woman's shape and came up behind Jennifer.

"Who calls me?" the Lady in White asked, her voice like a wisp of wind. "Who curses my ain?"

Jennifer whirled about. This close, Mary MacFadden was almost solid, though as white as a marble statue. She had regular features that didn't quite add up to beauty but certainly had charm. Only her eyes were dark, emitting no light.

Jennifer was surprised at how calm she felt in the ghost's presence. Not frightened at all.

"Who called?" the Lady in White said.

Suddenly Jennifer *was* frightened. Somehow the ghost had heard her. Her knees began to tremble.

"I suppose I called you," she told the ghost. "And I meant it when I said your brother's a pig." She wondered briefly if that was a smart thing to say. After all, she didn't want to make the ghost angry. *But it's the truth,* she thought. *Andrew MacFadden is a pig!* And just as suddenly, she wasn't afraid anymore.

"Your brother kept a message from you all those years ago, as you know, and he *still* won't give it up. But he told us the secret without meaning to, back at our house. He said, 'In the stane a token of luv. Three from the bottom and four above.' Do you know what that means?"

It had been two hundred and fifty years, after all. Iain the piper had forgotten. What if Mary's memory hadn't lasted that long, either?

For a moment, a shadow passed over that shadow face, a quick flicker, and then gone. "Och, aye—I remember. The token in the stane wasna there. I looked at the time, but it wasna there." She shook her head. "Nae, that's nae richt. There's something else troubling me." She gave a sad little shadow smile.

"Where is the stane?" Jennifer asked again.

"Our stane," Mary MacFadden whispered. Then she turned away and ran like the haar, like the sea mist, over the brown scrub grass to the back side of the little church, her feet never touching the ground.

Jennifer had a hard time keeping up. But she got to the church just as Mary MacFadden was counting the stones.

"One, two, three." She was going left to right along the bottom of a set of stones that was all but hidden behind a small stand of broom. Then she counted four up from there and placed her white hand over that stone. The stone was covered with a fuzzing of green lichen and moss.

"Here." Her hand was as insubstantial as the rest of her. She turned with a puzzled expression and said to Jennifer, "But I canna seem to open it."

Jennifer gawped at her. "Open a stone?"

"Noo I recall it. On the day Iain went off wi'oot a word, I came here to find if he'd left me something in our stane. We always left things here. A rose. A ribbon. A white pebble. Tokens of our luv. But never luv notes. He couldna write, ye see. Or read. But I couldna slide the stane open. It had been harled over, and I couldna put my hand in." Dark tears ran down her cheeks. "And then he was gone forever."

Gone forever.

The words burned in Jennifer's mind. If she didn't get the stone open in time, Peter would be gone forever, too.

"Let me try!" Jennifer's fingers scrabbled without success on the stone.

She could hear the piper and Peter quarreling outside the gate. She could hear Gran's voice trying to quiet them. The dog was suddenly howling. Only the horse was still.

And then the church bell began its inexorable toll.

Midnight had begun.

FOURTEEN

Midnight Magic

Jennifer pushed at the top of the stone and at the bottom. She hammered with the heel of her fist in the middle. She tried to pry around the edges — top, bottom, sides. Nothing worked. The harled stone wouldn't move.

Her fingers hurt from trying.

And the bell kept tolling.

Think, she told herself. *Slow down, Jennifer, and think. This is magic, not stonemasonry.*

She hadn't a sledgehammer or a steel levering bar. And she doubted that the piper would lend her his ghostly sword.

"What else?" she whispered to herself. "What else beats stone?"

Meow.

She looked down at her feet. The white cat was sitting there, slowly washing its back leg.

"How did you get in?" Then she remembered that she'd left the iron gate ajar just a sliver.

The cat left off washing its hind leg and looked into the distance, through the Lady in White. She put out a white paw.

Jennifer remembered the cat making just that motion earlier, when Molly and she had been playing Stone, Scissors, Paper. "Of course!"

Stone breaks scissors.

Scissors cut paper.

And paper...

"Covers stone," she whispered. "I need paper." Then she remembered the piece of notebook paper in her pocket, the one with all the notes about ghosts and green ladies and banshees scribbled on it.

"This had better work," she told the cat, because she knew she didn't have time for anything else. The midnight toll was going relentlessly on.

Reaching into her pocket, she pulled out the paper and placed it carefully over the stone—third from the bottom and four from above.

The paper fit exactly.

Then she leaned her weight against the paper, whispering passionately, "Paper covers stone. Paper covers stone. Paper covers..."

Her hand suddenly slipped into the stone as if the stone were made of not-quite-jelled Jell-O; cold Jell-O, two hundred or more years cold.

She gave herself no time to be amazed. She *had* no time for anything but action. The midnight bell was still tolling, though she'd lost count of how many chimes had actually rung.

Feeling around, her fingers touched something inside the stone, something that was hard and round. Carefully she drew the token out. When she was entirely free of the jelly-stone, she stepped away, wiping her hand on her shirt.

The paper floated to the ground.

She looked at what she held in her hand. It was a ring of gold, with an inscription encircling the outside. Holding the ring up toward the moonlight, she managed to read: "Even death will nae part us."

"I think," said Jennifer, turning, "that this belongs to you." She held the ring out to the Lady in White.

Mary MacFadden took the ring, read the inscription, and for the first time smiled. "He said that often. He must hae told the goldsmith what to write." Her eyes lost their black shroud look and reflected the moonlight.

Jennifer thought, *I was wrong about her. She's very beautiful.*

And then the bell rang again.

"Hurry," Jennifer said to the ghost. "Oh, please, Mary MacFadden—hurry!"

The Lady in White turned and ran toward the piper, her small feet inches above the ground. Not a blade of grass moved as she passed over.

"Gran—open the gate!" Jennifer cried. "Open it. She's got the token, she's got the ring."

Gran's head jerked up. She said something to the piper, spun about, and pushed open the gate. And all of them—piper, Peter, Gran, the dog, and the horse—raced into the graveyard.

Peter was fast, but the piper was faster. He met Mary MacFadden by her gravestone. Picking her up in his arms, he twirled her around and around till her skirts billowed out and made a soft *shusssh*-ing. He kissed her brow and then her nose and then both her cheeks.

They broke apart and stared at each other and laughed, the sound suddenly louder and more perfect than any tolling bell.

Then the piper set the Lady in White down carefully, as if she were made of precious glass—*for surely,* Jennifer thought, *she's no longer flesh and bone.* He slipped the ring onto her finger.

"Even death," he mouthed to her, "will nae part us."

Mary MacFadden turned then and, glancing over her shoulder, addressed Peter.

"I fergive ye, Andrew," she cried. "Yer my brother, my twin soul, and I fergive ye from the bottom o' my heart. Ye meant fer the best, but ye were wrong then. And yer wrong noo." She turned back to Iain and raised her beautiful, shining face to him.

He bent down to her and kissed her again, though this time on the mouth, first lightly, and then with a great passion.

At the moment of the kiss, the two literally became one, their ghostly shapes coalescing into a white pillar of mist that rose higher and higher, until it was lost against the whiteness of the solstice moon.

Jennifer felt hot tears cascading down her cheeks as she watched them, and she cried out, "You're safe, Peter. Safe."

Just then the horse whinnied, the dog howled, and Gran cried out, "No, Jennie lass. No."

Jennifer turned then and saw that it was not

Peter staring out at her but the furious eyes of Andrew MacFadden.

"What hae ye done, ye meddlesome lass? Ye've lost me my ain sister." He raised a fist to strike her.

And the last bell of midnight tolled.

At that very moment, a hubbub began outside the gates, as if hundreds of people were suddenly gathering there. A mob of them.

Peter put his head back and laughed grimly. "As ye lost me my sister, so I'll tak yer brother frae yer side. The Sluagh is come, and I'll gae wi' them. Ye'll ne'er see me again."

"The Sluagh?" It was one of the words on her piece of paper. Desperately she tried to remember what the Sluagh was.

"The grim parade o' the dead," the dog shouted. "Jennifer lass—dinna let the madman oot."

But Peter had already started for the gate, faster than Jennifer or Gran or the dog.

Only the horse could still get there in time. He barreled ahead of Peter, his mighty hooves gouging divots out of the brown grass. Then he slammed his great shoulder against the gate. As his shoulder touched the ironwork, he flung his head back and screamed. It was an awful, high-pitched sound that seemed so unlikely coming from such a large animal.

A magic creature can't touch cold iron, Jennifer thought, remembering the burn mark on the dog's back. *Oh, horse, oh, Thunder, how badly have you been hurt?*

Thunder limped away from the gate and stood, shuddering, by the wall. But he'd done what he'd set out to do, and the gate was closed.

Jennifer could smell the singed hair and burnt flesh all the way from where she stood.

"Lucky I've brought my unguent," Gran said as she walked over to the horse. She opened her purse "There'll be a great need fer it this nicht." The horse trembled slightly as she began to rub the oily stuff into his burnt skin.

Peter stopped by the ironwork gate, hands at his sides. He put his head back and howled. It was a worse sound than any the horse had made, and the little hairs on the back of Jennifer's neck stood straight up.

But that howl didn't stop the progress of the Sluagh, the doomed souls, who marched in a grim, shuffling line beyond the cemetery walls.

Forgiveness

By the time Jennifer got to the gate, half the Sluagh had passed by. But there were still plenty for her to see, a long twisting line of doomed souls slumping along.

There were soldiers in kilts with swords sticking out of their chests. A woman with a noose around her neck, eyes bulging wide. A mother and two children horribly burnt, the puckered scars still red and raw. Three men in long black coats and white collars, thin garrotes encircling their necks. Two women in ball gowns with broken bottles in their hands. A farmer in a slouched hat, a knife in his eye. A fisherman in a bright yellow slicker, half his face eaten away.

There were hundreds of others, all equally, horribly dead. As they marched along, they were accompanied by a strange babble, of which Jennifer could occasionally understand a word—of pain, of horror, of regret.

She turned away. Her stomach and chest were tight, the way she felt right before getting sick. She was afraid she might throw up, and she didn't dare. Not here. Not now.

Instead, she sought Gran's eyes.

"Look away, Jennifer, 'tis nae a sight fer a bairn," Gran said, as she massaged the burn ointment into the horse's shoulder.

"Who are they, Gran?" Jennifer said in a whisper.

"They're the unshriven dead, the unburied, the unmourned and unloved. Those who killed themselves or were left to die alone, by accident or by design. Dinna look more, Jennie lass. If ye do, they can call ye oot, and then ye'll have to gae wi' them. And I couldna bear that."

But Jennifer was no longer looking at the Sluagh. Instead, she was staring at Peter, for he'd turned away from the sight of the marching dead, too, and was weeping loudly, his hands over his face.

"Mary forgave you, you know," Jennifer said to him. "She loved you as much as a twin can love. Closer than ordinary brother and sister. I know. I'm a twin, too. But Mary had another life—as the piper's own true love. You denied her that."

Peter nodded and took his hands down from his face. That face was old, lined, haggard. "But how *could* she fergive? I lied to her. I harled over her token. When McGregor never came back, she died o' her grief, thinking he'd never cared fer her. And I, who had killed her, died wi' her, though I lived on forty more years and had a family o' my ain who begged fer the love I couldna give them. Forty more years preaching God's words, and I the biggest sinner o' them a'." His fists went to his temples.

Taking his hands in hers, Jennifer said, "If God can forgive you and your sister can forgive you, surely *you* can forgive yourself, Andrew Mac-Fadden."

He looked at her with hooded eyes. With tired eyes. "Fergive mysel? And how do I do that, lass?"

"On your knees, I guess," Jennifer said. She pointed dramatically to the ground. "On your knees."

He sank to his knees and held his hands up toward the sky or toward heaven or toward the place where his sister had disappeared. Jennifer was never to know exactly which.

"I do repent o' my wickedness, Lord," he said. "And if Mary can fergive me, then I do fergive myself as weel." Suddenly he pitched forward onto his face, and lay there stiffly as the sun rose over the eastern cemetery wall at three-thirty in the morning.

Three hours had passed so quickly. It was morning already.

Morning. Too late, then, Jennifer thought. She couldn't move. Not an inch. She felt as if she'd been cast in stone. Harled stone.

Just then, the dog came over and started licking the back of Peter's neck, his great tongue sloshing up into the hairline and then down under Peter's collar.

Peter shuddered and sat up. "Leave me alone," he cried, pushing the dog away roughly. "You're wetting me all over, you snot rag!"

"Not till ye fergive me," cried the dog. "I put ye in danger. And all because..."

"Peter!" Jennifer cried. "You're back. Oh my gosh—it worked! It worked!" Unbidden tears began cascading down her cheeks. She wiped them away with her fists.

Peter looked puzzled. "What worked? Have I been away?" He got to his knees. "Why do girls always cry at the silliest things? And when are we going to see the ghosts, Jen? I thought that's why we came out here."

"You idiot—you were a ghost yourself," Jennifer said. "We thought we'd lost you. And it's the night after the first time we came here."

"Will ye both fergive me?" the dog howled.

They looked at him, and Jennifer said, "Forgive for *what*?"

Peter added, "Spill it, dog. This had better be good."

The dog groveled at their feet and whimpered. "It's nae a pretty tale."

"Pretty or not," Jennifer said, "out with it."

"Aye, yer richt. Best said than sorry." He nodded his head, ears flopping. "The piper McGregor was my master, and I followed him to war. I was loyal, see. Dogs are. It was a lang, cold jog we had. Mile after mile of it. But when the battle itself came— the sleet, the drums, the pipes, the screams—och, how I ran. Freely do I admit it noo. I ran and ran all the way back hame, where I bumped into the wizard Michael Scot, who was moving forward in time. He kenned me, he did, kenned me fer a coward. It seemed to please him."

Peter said in a stunned voice. "McGregor? Battle? What has that to do with anything?"

Gran had come over and heard the confession, too. Hands on hips, she glared at the dog. "So when ye kenned they were twins—Peter and Jennifer—and heard the ghostly bagpipes playing, ye thought to mak amends with yer auld master, is that it?"

The dog hung his head. "Yes, yes." He whimpered. "I never thought to hurt young Peter."

"Well, nae harm's done that doesna leave a scar," Gran said. "Besides, all's well noo. Fer all o' us. Even ye, ye greetin, self-abusing hound. Confession's gud fer the soul, they say."

"*If* dogs have souls," Jennifer added angrily.

"Och, they do that," Gran said. "All living things do. It was what interested Michael Scot in him, o' course." She reached into her purse and pulled out the handkerchief again. "I wonder how much himsel's had a hand in today's doings?"

Just then Thunder limped over to them, the cat fast asleep on his broad back.

124 ■ The Bagpiper's Ghost

Peter didn't seem to be listening. Instead, he was staring at Gran and the horse with its burnt shoulder, and the sleeping cat. His jaw gaped open. "What are *they* doing here, Jen? Did you let them know? You shouldn't have done that. It was supposed to be a secret."

"I'll tell you everything later," said Jennifer. "But let's get back home first. I'm *starving*."

"That's funny—I'm starving, too," Peter said. "I feel as if I haven't eaten for a day at least."

She laughed. "You haven't."

"No, really," Peter said. "I always feel what you feel. That's what being a twin's all about, I guess."

"Something like that," she agreed, smiling. Then she held out her hand and yanked him to his feet. They headed for the gate, the dog trotting placidly and silently at Peter's side.

"We had better study more aboot twin magic," Gran said to Thunder. "Power is power, but double is trouble. We might nae be so lucky next time."

The cat opened one sleepy eye in comment. Then horse, cat, and old woman followed the twins through the gate and home.

.

A Scottish Glossary

aboot—about
ain—own
auld—old
awa—away
bairges—struts
bairns—children
bawties—rabbits
besom—woman, often a talkative one
blethering—talking nonsense
bodie—body, person
bonnie—handsome or lovely
by my fegs—a mild oath, like "Rats!"
canny—smart, knowing
carlin—witch, old woman
clout—a rag or cloth
conies—rabbits
coof—fool, simpleton
daftie—crazy person
dinna—do not
doited—crazed, enfeebled, foolish
doon—down
dorty—stubborn
forenoon—morning
fou—drunk
fowsome—filthy, impure, obscene
frae—from

gae—go

going my dinger—going about vigorously

gormless—stupid

greetin teenie—someone who is always complaining

gud—good

haar—sea mist

hae—have

hame—home

harling—roughcasting to protect soft stone from the weather

hoovering—vacuuming, or slang for vigorously eating (Hoover is a brand of vacuum cleaner.)

ken—know

kirk—church, usually Protestant

lad—boy

lang—long

lass—girl

licht—light

losh—a mild swear word, like "gosh"

luv—love

mair—more

mischant—worthless person

nae—not, no

nicht—night

noo—now

oot—out

paidling—aimless, feckless

porridge—oatmeal

puir—poor
richt—right
shut your cake hole—shut your mouth
spoacher—a poacher, thief
stane—stone
swick—to deceive
toom-headit—brainless, empty-headed
toon—town
weans—little children
wee—small, little
weel—well
wee, sleekit, timorous, cowerin—from a Robert Burns
    poem, "To a Mouse," it means "small, sly,
    frightened, cowering"
wi'oot—without
wouldna—would not